LITTLE GEMS

LITTLE GEMS

A collection of short stories

by **Ray Stone**

Little Gems

A Collection of Short Stories

Formatting and Cover Design — Anthony Smits

Contents

IN THE LAW
WE TRUST

A cautionary tale of how a successful man's idyllic life is turned into a nightmare because of a humanitarian cause and an affliction few of us experience - an affliction that can often play havoc with one's mind through fear of the unknown.

The clock on the wall showed 23.55. The long red hand paused briefly with a sharp staccato tick, accompanied by an almost undetectable shiver each time it measured a second.

Paul Devereux heard the curtain pulled back and muffled spontaneous applause from behind the screen as the Warden replaced the receiver on the wall phone and pressed the intercom button next to it. A short buzz sounded from a small room next door to the chamber.

Devereux felt a slight calming sensation as the sedative entered his body, relaxing muscles and releasing the tension. Within a minute, his eyelids were flickering. Thoughts of loved ones, mental pictures of treasured moments, all flashed through his mind. Seconds later, he was unconscious.

***

Professor Devereux looked pleased with himself, and not without good cause. The interview went well and tomorrow's papers would carry the story. The abolition of capital punishment was a long way off but still gathering momentum. His views were well-known nationally, and after several months of hard investigative work, he had achieved the near impossible. He was instrumental in proving that the State of Alabama wrongly executed a man convicted on circumstantial evidence of murder. Devereux was a cause celebre.

Unfortunately, he attracted many enemies along the way including police officers who openly threatened him. Hate mail filled his post box daily. Several times on T.V. the D.A's office ridiculed him and dismissed him as a crank. He was used to that. The more they threw at him, the more he liked it. They were on the defensive.

Devereux had held center stage at the interview. With overwhelming evidence showing incompetence on the part of the prosecution, the District Attorney admitted that his office got it wrong.

Making his way back to his dressing room, Devereux reflected on his success. The only regret was that Chantelle, his wife, was not with him to share in his triumph. She was a lifelong supporter of abolition, but just as recognition started to come his way, she died, sadly, of cancer, just eight months after diagnosis. It was sudden and a great shock to him. Heartbroken, he retired from his law practice and became reclusive.

It was three years later that some of his old friends insisted he take up lecturing again on the university circuit. His knowledge of the law and the criminal mind made him one of the most respected authorities in his field. After deliberating for a month, he decided to start campaigning again and was soon being quoted throughout mass media.

He sat in a chair in front of the mirror in his dressing room while the makeup assistant, Dana, attended to his face for a few minutes, cleaning off the cream and powder.

"You ought to get a good night's sleep," she said, her big brown eyes studying him in the mirror. "Those lines under your eyes are ugly."

Devereux picked up a comb and held it out for her. "I know, but at least I do not have to look after my good looks, do I?"

She laughed. "Well, I don't know. You look very distinguished to me."

"That's another way of saying I'm going bald and gray."

They laughed as he got up from the chair.

"Here's your coat, professor. I think you're gonna need it tonight. The weather forecast warned of rain."

After saying goodnight, Devereux made his way downstairs to the reception area. He stood for a moment at the main entrance before deciding to walk home through the park. The exercise would do him good, and in any case, the T.V station was not far from where he lived.

Walking down the steps outside the studio, Devereux felt several light spots of rain on his head. Opening his umbrella and then his stick, he stepped to the edge of the sidewalk and paused, listening for traffic.

Born blind, he was used to getting around the city he had been brought up in. Always preferring the little folding stick to a guide dog, he could travel around Birmingham as quickly as anyone else. The rain increased.

Passing traffic hissed in the downfall. Devereux walked across the road carefully. The Town Hall clock chimed the hour, eleven o'clock. Thinking that he might be in time to catch the eleven-forty newscast, he hurried to be in time to listen to it.

Reaching the park gates, he turned into the pathway that led through some trees to the playground and beyond. The wind blew in gusts, pushing the swings back and forth. They squeaked noisily above the rustle of the leafy trees that surrounded the playground.

A dog somewhere in the distance barked. An impatient driver amongst the night-time traffic on the other side of the park hooted a horn.

Birds rose and flapped out of a tree in front of him, startling Devereux. He stopped and listened intently. Then he heard it. Clearly audible above the blustery wind there came a muffled cough followed by the flip top clack of a Zippo lighter being snapped shut.

Devereux started to walk again and passing the trees at the end of the play area, he smelled smoke. Curious, he wondered why someone would want to stop and smoke in such inclement weather. Perhaps, he thought, it was just a kid.

After another fifty yards, the path sloped gently downward and evened out as it reached the edge of a small lake. Many years before, when Chantelle first brought him to the lake after their engagement, they walked every pathway while she described the beauty of the trees, the flowers, rockeries, and lakes. They sat by the lake many times during the years that followed, eating lunch and relaxing. Now, during Spring and Summer mainly, he sat in their seat by the lake, remembering.

Devereux's thoughts were ended abruptly. Someone was following. He could not mistake the sound of heavy footsteps on the gravel a short way behind. Whoever it was seemed to be keeping pace with him. He felt a little uneasy and slowed to allow the stranger to catch up and pass. He listened, aware that his heart was beating faster. The follower had stopped. The only sound above the wind was the rustling leaves.

Since childhood, one thing always frightened him. Being followed. Standing quite still, he heard someone cough. Worried in case he was being followed by a mugger, he walked on quickly, tapping his stick from side to side more urgently.

Footsteps crunched on the ground behind him again. He felt like shouting out but thought better of it. If he shouted, he might be attacked before he reached safety. There again he might make a fool of himself. It could be some kid playing around.

Trying hard not to act scared, he hurried on to the park exit opposite the all-night shopping mall. If he could make an exit, he would be safe among the shoppers and late night diners. By now his heart was pounding against his chest, and despite the cold wind, his shirt was becoming damp.

His stick touched the bin near the end of the path. He breathed with relief. A few yards more and he would be at the exit. Relieved at the moment and lost in his anxiety to reach safety, he forgot the protruding stone base of the drinking fountain the other side of the bin. His foot caught the base, and he fell heavily. Grabbing for his stick, he felt the umbrella fly away, captured by a gust of wind. There was a loud cough. He froze, panic welling up inside him.

"What do you want?" Devereux sobbed.

There was no reply. He sat sobbing for a few seconds and

then picked himself up. Soaking wet, he rose unsteadily to his feet and made his way through the exit to the safety of the sidewalk. No-one followed him.

Across the street, the mall was busy, mostly with people using the precinct as a shortcut and shelter from the rain. Devereux decided this was the safest thing for him to do. The mall was well illuminated, and once through to the far end, he would be just two blocks from his apartment. From the far end, he could hail a cab.

Breathing heavily, he crossed the street. His clothes were wet with mud and sweat was running down his forehead. Some grazed skin on his hands stung. He stopped just inside the mall entrance and felt a little safer. He brushed his coat and wiped his face with the back of a hand while trying to compose himself.

The thick aroma of burgers filled his nostrils. McDonalds was open and by the sounds of things, very busy. He remembered something and smiled. There were some telephones just inside the restaurant. He would call the Sheriff's department and get them to send a patrolman to see him home. There was sure to be a squad car nearby.

Devereux felt better for having a plan of action, and walked into the restaurant to find the telephones. He picked up a receiver and called the Sheriff's department. After explaining his predicament to an understanding and sympathetic officer, he was asked to give his name and address.

There was a pause. Then, "Excuse me, sir, did you say, Devereux, Professor Paul Devereux?"

"Yes, that's me. I'm on my way home from the T.V. studios."

The line went silent for a while. Devereux hoped they would send a car.

Moments later the officer was back online. "Professor, I'm very sorry, but unless the person or persons who may or may not be following you actually abuse you in any way, either physically or verbally, there is not a lot we can do."

Devereux lost his temper, attracting attention from the diners. "Listen, you idiot, I've been followed. My life may be in danger. For God's sake, can't you do anything?"

"I'm sorry, professor, but our officers are busy right now." The voice was polite but firm.

"If I were someone else you'd be here in a couple of minutes, you bastard!"

Devereux started to shout. "You don't like the truth. You don't like it when you're shown up on T.V. You wait and see. I'll make you pay for this."

There was a click, and the line went dead. Devereux slammed the receiver down and was aware that the diners had gone quiet. Embarrassed, he turned to walk out and collided with someone coming through the door. Customers started to laugh. He was making a fool of himself.

"Sorry," said a man, "allow me."

The door opened, and Devereux was guided out into

the mall. As the door closed, the man coughed. It was an unmistakable cough. Devereux flushed hot and cold. His hands shook. He had to get away. With stick flailing from side to side, he almost ran down the mall, bumping into people along the way.

At the end of the mall, he turned left and stopped, out of breath. He knew that a covered cab rank which stood a few yards away closed at midnight. His index finger urgently touched the face of his wristwatch. It was eleven twenty-five. Wearily climbing into the back of a cab, he gave his address to the driver. He closed his eyes and silently cursed his decision to walk.

Several minutes later the cab pulled up outside the apartment block. Devereux, by now a little calmer, paid the driver and climbed the steps to the main door of the block.

Once inside his apartment, he made straight for the shower. He ached all over and was shivering with the cold. The exertions of the last hour had exhausted him completely. While he was undressing, he decided to write to the Police Commissioner in the morning and complain about the treatment he had received. He stood under the shower and let the hot water soothe his aching limbs.

***

The sidewalk glistened under the street lights. Rain continued to fall. A cigarette dropped into the gutter with a hiss. From under one of the trees that lined the side of the boulevard came a muffled cough. Brad Miller had been standing there sheltering from the rain ever since a cab dropped him off. He looked up at the block and decided to wait a little longer. A crumpled pack of Camels was poking out of his top jacket pocket. He leaned against the tree, took a cigarette from the pack and lit it with the Zippo.

This would be the third mark in a week and the easiest. No need to follow and then return to break in when the victim was out. The old man was different. Miller did not know how he was going to break in, but it was a challenge that would give him a buzz just for the hell of it. Even if the man did wake up, so what? He could not see anyone so he could not finger anyone. He'd played cat and mouse with the blind man all night and scared him a couple of times, especially at McDonalds. He liked to scare people. It was fun.

Fifteen minutes later he slipped across the boulevard to the apartment block and bounded silently up the entrance steps two at a time. He pulled a thin piece of mica board from his jeans and opened the door in seconds. He crept into the lobby. After feeling along the line of post boxes on the wall, he found what he wanted and smiled. There was a brass plate on one box with the apartment number indented on it. Miller climbed the stairs carefully.

Up on the third floor, all was still. The only noise came from the rain beating persistently on the window panes at the end of the corridor. To one side of the window sat an old wooden chair, placed in the corner. Miller picked it up and positioned it up against the door of apartment 117.

Climbing onto the chair, he reached up to the small oblong window above the door frame. The window was open a couple of inches. Expert hands pushed the window inward and up. With a little piece of cardboard taken from his pocket, Miller folded it into a wedge. This he then put into place on one side between the window and the frame. A gap of eighteen inches was enough to give him access into the apartment.

Holding onto the bottom of the frame, he pulled himself up until he was able to grab a sprinkler pipe that ran along the length of the ceiling. With both hands gripping the pipe, he swung himself up and slid both feet through the gap until his body was halfway into the apartment. With ease, he twisted himself around until his stomach rested on the window frame. The wedge was then removed, and the window returned to its original position as he dropped silently to the floor inside the apartment.

Miller carefully opened the door, picked up the chair, and replaced it to the landing corner. Preoccupied with his work, he did not notice a figure hiding in the shadows of the stairway as he returned to 117. A hand grabbed him from behind. Instinctively, Miller turned and punched his would-be captor hard in the face.

"You son of a bitch!" came a gruff voice.

They grappled with each other, punching and kicking until Miller broke loose. He swung wildly at the other man who, trying to avoid a punch, slumped back against the apartment door. Miller, coughing loudly, kicked the man in the ribs and made good his escape.

***

Devereux woke with a start. A loud crash was followed by someone coughing. His worst nightmare was coming true. He began to shake, his stomach churning. With short, shallow breaths, he sat upright in bed and reached for the bedside table drawer. His hand fumbled frantically inside. His fingers finally felt metal, and he withdrew a long thin-bladed letter knife that he kept there for emergencies.

He slid out of bed and moved to one side of the bedroom door where he could hide if it opened. Trembling, he stood with heart racing, waiting. It was quiet.

Then he heard them.

Footsteps were coming toward him—slow, deliberate footsteps. The door handle squeaked. Devereux tensed, his nerves at breaking point. Terrified, he felt a cold draft of air as the door slowly opened. It was too much for him. He lunged forward with the paper knife.

"There, you bastard," he screamed hysterically, "take that!"

They both fell to the floor, Devereux plunging the knife

again and again. Anger and violence poured from him. Exhausted, he finally lay on top of the body, crying, unable to move. When the moment of initial shock receded, he picked himself up and stumbled into the living room to call the Sheriff's department.

He remembered his last call to the Sheriff's office, regretting that they had not been more helpful. If they had, things would have not gone so far. He dropped the knife on the carpet and reached for the phone.

It was ten minutes later that Detectives found Devereux slumped in an armchair. He was covered in blood. The paper knife was laying on the carpet by his feet.

They listened to his story that he was followed home by the intruder. After he had finished, Devereux had to go over his story again to make sure no detail had been overlooked.

Several hours later, downtown, during his interview, Devereux was played a recording of his earlier abusive and threatening call to the Sheriff's Department, which he'd made because they refused to help him after he reported being followed by a suspected mugger.

As far as the detectives were concerned, there was no sign of forced entry to the apartment block or Devereux's apartment. As for the intruder laying on Devereux's floor; after being called by the Sheriff and asked to do a favor, retired deputy, Marvin Tucks, living on the ground floor had looked in to see if the professor was alright.

The detectives surmised that Devereux, annoyed at Tucks disturbing his sleep and thinking the Sheriff's Department was harassing him, had viciously attacked and slain the deputy in a rage. No other intruder figured in the incident. Devereux, they suggested, was too clever for his own good. Devereux was charged with murder.

***

Brad Miller sat on a bar stool and looked up at the T.V. lunchtime news. A picture of Devereux flashed up on the screen. It was announced that the professor was executed at midnight the day before at Oaksville Penitentiary.

CONDURROW

The tin mines of Cornwall are gone.

Ghostly piles of brick and old smelting furnace stacks still pepper the landscape. What stories they hide of the suffering poor mining families and the child laborers.

Mrs Malock's eyes widened. "Silas Dench will be turning in the sod. A fire all night is unheard of in this ghostly pile of morbid bricks."

With some impatience, I sat watching a gathering dawn slowly turn blackness into a thousand shapes as the sun crept above the distant hills and glimmered and twinkled through the leafy forest. Since Mr. Aloysius Crumley's letter had arrived the previous week, its contents had given me cause for some concern. I found it hard to sleep let alone wait for the Friday, the day he said I should call on him at his London office in Cranley Square.

My journey from Denton Bowes had been tiring for my horse, Caz, but nothing could dull my excitement as I rode him along the bridle path, counting the milestones. I was to report to 'Crumley and Beddingborn,' solicitors to the gentry and commissioners of oaths at precisely 9.00 on the morning. There was no indication as to the nature of the business Mr. Crumley wished to discuss with me save a hint that news of the death of a distant relative was indeed to my advantage.

With Caz rested, I rode the last few miles into London and arrived at Cranley Square as the bell in St Stephens Tower chimed 9.00.

***

Mr. Crumley was a portly gentleman of old age who despite the advance in modern bespoke tailoring and the new Victorian fashion for short curled hair, persisted in wearing a powdered wig together with morning coat, breeches, and white stockings. With his large red jowled cheeks, squat nose and small piercing blue eyes, one would be forgiven for likening him to a jolly fine pig.

"Come in Master Jeddler, come in and warm yourself by the fire."

With a kindly hand on my shoulder, he ushered me

gently into a large red leather wing chair in front of a roaring log fire opposite his large oak desk. Despite being backlit from the dimpled windows that looked down on the noisy square below, two large candles standing on a bookcase were still alight. The aroma of candle wax and Mr. Crumley's snuff wafted across the office.

"Now Arthur," Crumley said, pulling his morning coat about his knees carefully as he sat, "you Sir are a man of substance through the passing of your dear mother some years ago."

My brow wrinkled. "I'm sorry, I don't understand."

"She would not have told you that you had an uncle, one Silas Dench and that due to a family tragedy which he was responsible for, they never spoke again. Your uncle wanted to make good and hired my services to draw up a will leaving his estate to you, on his death."

"And as he is now deceased his estate comes to me?" I asked.

Crumley beamed. "Yes, you are now the owner of a tin mine in Cornwall together with the house and two thousand guineas."

I looked into the dancing flames of the fire. "Will you tell me about the tragedy?"

"No. Your mother kept it from you and Silas from me. You must to travel to Cornwall and unravel that dark mystery for yourself."

With great excitement, I left Mr. Crumley's office and set

about putting my business in order and, after two hectic days, I took delivery of one large leather chest containing all my belongings, sent by night coach from Denton Bowes.

Later, as I boarded the Hansom Cab for Paddington station outside the King's Head, the innkeeper's large, jovial wife hurriedly pushed a small picnic parcel, tied up neatly with a red and white cloth, into my hands while my leather chest was loaded.

"Eleven hours stopping at all stations and only two stops for your ablutions, master Jeddler. You'll need the food to calm your nerves."

Shadbroke, the innkeeper, shook his large bald head and placed both hands on his hips. "Iron steam trains...whatever next. You mark my words, they won't last. They scare the horses too much."

An hour later I found myself sitting comfortably inside a brightly decorated Great Western Railway carriage. Two years earlier, in 1867, a new through train service began running the three hundred and thirty miles to Penzance twice a day.

With a small advance of twenty pounds from Mr. Crumley, I decided to spend six pounds and ten pence on a first class ticket. Sitting in the second class open carriages in October meant an uncomfortable journey, especially in inclement weather. The leather seats were comforting, and without wind or rain to disturb me, I settled into an adventurous mood.

"Are you going all the way, Sir?"

Thoughts of my recent activities evaporated immediately as a gruff voice drew my gaze from the passing autumnal countryside.

"Yes," I replied, smiling broadly. "Arthur Jeddler."

"Edwin Malby." He offered long bony fingers that gripped me tightly as we shook.

My companion was an elderly gentleman dressed smartly in a morning coat. On his lap lay a copy of 'The Times' and by his side, on the next seat, a splendid top hat. He raised his hand slowly and brushed a rather fine white handle-bar moustache, first one way and then the other, with an upturned knuckle.

His dark eyes looked steadily into mine. "You are in business, then."

It was more an observation rather than an inquiry as he studied my attire, nodding.

"Tin, Sir," I stated cheerfully. "An inheritance ... I am to inspect my mine and profit from it hopefully."

The man's demeanor changed, giving me cause for concern. His eyes narrowed, half covered as they did so by thick bushy eyebrows. He tapped the newspaper on his lap and then pointed a trembling finger.

"Great Condurrow. News of you posted here, Sir. A cursed affair, Sir ... a cursed affair," he retorted.

Taken aback, I asked politely for an explanation as to his

concern.

"I chair the 'Amalgamated Tin Mine Association.'

Silas Dench was a greedy man, his memory stained with the suffering of so many he failed to care for properly."

Despite further attempts to draw more from him, he preferred to snap the newspaper open with a loud crack and bury his head behind it.

A still dark cloud quickly descended, enveloping me for the rest of the journey as we clattered along the rails.

The train arrived on time after dark at 7.30 despite adverse weather. Edwin Malby left with a warning and a somewhat disappointing surprise for me as he stepped lightly down from the carriage.

"Sir, you would do well not to emulate your predecessor's practices if you decide to reopen Great Condurrow." He sniffed loudly and marched off into a gathering mist, gently swinging his walking cane.

The bumpy coach ride from Penzance station to Mullions Cove was, to say the least, a dismal and bitterly cold journey. For two hours I shivered, despite a thick overcoat, as the coachman labored to keep the horses veering sideways over deep waterlogged ruts. The short conversation and warning from Malby added to my discomfort. I tried to put the man from my mind and longed for a hot meal and a warm bed.

**

Condurrow House sat atop a cliff overlooking the angry Atlantic some twenty or more miles along the coast. After two grueling hours, it came into view as we rounded a bend in the carriageway. Large and imposing with one side of the house rising from the very edge of the clifftop, chimney stacks pointed upwards like bony fingers clawing at the dark sky.

As the coach left me, I stood with my travel chest by my side looking up at the house. It looked bleak and uninviting, the grey walls emanating a sense of solitude edged with menace. The large oak door swung inwards with a loud squeak, and a dancing shaft of light from flickering gas lamps on the wood-paneled entrance walls washed over me.

"There's no-one to help with your chest, and I am long past the age to help. Shift yourself in and be quick or the frosted air will suck the warmth from the hall."

The silhouette of a tall, thin woman stood in the doorway with hands on hips. I picked up my chest and trod heavily up the steps and past the woman. With a loud bang and clattering iron latch, the door closed behind me.

"I'm Mrs. Malocks, housekeeper for the last twenty-five years, so don't go changing things unless you want the back of me."

Mrs. Malocks stood in a black dress with arms folded loosely, sharp unblinking eyes looking me over. Her white hair stood up, tied tightly in a bun; her small hooked nose and shallow cheeks giving her a haughty appearance that made me wary. She was not a woman, I thought, who stood any nonsense.

"There's a candle on the table. Snuff it when you go to bed. We don't waste wax here. It costs too much." She pointed toward the stairs. "And your room is the last along the top landing. You'll find a fire in the grate and food by your bed. I'm here when you wake."

"Thank you," I muttered quietly.

I trod the stairs slowly, carrying my chest. Each step creaked with defiance.

At the top, I rested on the landing. The passage before me was full of moving shadows that were accompanied by a howling wind outside that rattled the long window's panes of glass.

The chill in my room had been replaced by warm air. The wooden latticed window by my bed spied out on a black ocean that silenced the howling wind each time it thunderously crashed against the cliffs below. Never in my excitement and expectations did I imagine I would feel so unwelcome.

I buried myself into the covers but could not shake the darkened mood I suffered. Determined to learn of Silas Dench, I fell asleep.

***

"Past five in the morning and you not risen. Silas Dench never lay after five, and if you're to catch the start of the shift, you'll be needing to taste tea and porridge by now."

Mrs. Malocks stood with her back to the cold grate with hands on hips, one foot beating the wooden floor in a quick little toe tap. A small tray, on which a bowl of steaming porridge and a large mug of tea stood, was placed on the nightstand by the side of my bed.

"Thank you, Mrs. Malocks." I shivered as I folded back the eiderdown and wrapped my hands around the mug. My breath spilled and disappeared quickly into the air after taking a sip. "Is it possible to bank the fire tonight for a warm room by dawn?" I asked.

Mrs. Malocks eyes widened. "Silas Dench will be turning in the sod. A fire all night is unheard of in this ghostly pile of morbid bricks." She nodded and left the room.

I finished the breakfast and washed hastily in the bowl of luke-warm water sitting on top of the dresser. Whatever else, my newly acquired housekeeper was efficient despite a noticeable lack of respect when referencing her previous employer. It seemed to me that through his own morbid existence, Silas Dench had left a dark and sad atmosphere within the house. I was sure, given Malocks remarks that my uncle was still present within the housekeeper's demeanor.

"Can I ask you about Silas Dench?" I said, entering the kitchen.

Mrs. Malocks sat at the kitchen table peeling potatoes by the light of a single gas lamp. A grey sky filled with fast-moving clouds was appearing on the dawn through the one small window that rattled continuously, buffeted by a strong wind that whistled through a crack in the wooden frame.

"There's not much to tell," she replied without looking from her work. "He was a mean man with a bad temper for sure."

"Did he not have a wife?"

Her fidgeting fingers stopped working and her head turned, tired but sharp eyes looking up into mine.

"That such a man could once be the kindest man on earth is hard to think of, but he was that. A beauty did capture his young heart, but your mother loved another despite the prospect of a better position in life. Silas' soul soured and darkened from then on and not a man nor woman ever shook him from his deep melancholy. He became a troubled and heartbroken man to the end."

"My mother?" I slumped into a chair, my heart beating with much force.

Mrs. Malocks gently touched my hand. "Your mother loved his brother, your pater, and not a word passed between the men after your mother married. When your father died, Silas paid for your boarding school and for your mother and her sister who lived with her to come here."

"So Uncle Silas boarded my mother and her sister here?"

32

"Nay lad, your mother still would not take him to her bed. Silas Dench cruelly sent them to work in the mine. It was the only way they could exist and was to be the death of both of them."

I remembered little of my mother except for my sadness at leaving her and my aunt shortly after father's death. His had been a long illness as I recalled, but I had no memories of family life. I was informed by my headmaster of my mother and aunt being killed in an accident. I returned home after leaving boarding school and started work as a clerk in the postal service.

I pulled the collar of my coat around my ears and leaving the broody house with a heavy heart, set out to visit the mine.

My first sight of the mine was with mixed emotion. A cluster of poorly maintained buildings surrounded the engine house. An unusually huge flywheel, some thirty feet high and attached to the engine, protruded from the back of the building through an open wall.

Two huge heavy beams moved in reciprocal motion on either side of the wheel and combined with other parts of which I had no knowledge, pumped water up from the bottom of the mine and returned it to the sea. Next to this crumbling brick house stood a tall stack that carried smoke from the smelting furnace.

About these buildings, the yard was unsurfaced with ash or stone, and bare earth had turned to a mud quagmire that rutted in all directions by ore wagons pulled by mules. Lack of maintenance or proper care, the area around each building was littered with old machinery and broken tools.

I found the mine office and entered. A small lantern illuminated a desk and, in its glow, the ruddy pot-marked face of Captain Pumblewood topped by a mass of untidy white hair looked down upon a small ledger. A row of yellowed teeth showed through thick chapped lips as he rose wearily to greet me with a smile. His coat was a grubby open naval three quarter, and two rows of silver buttons still adorned the breast. His trousers were caked in mud at the bottom half as were his boots. His white shirt was the only clean part of him.

"And you be Mr. Jeddler." He grinned and shook hands warmly. "I knows you were coming so I'll walk you smartly around."

I walked carefully, following him across the muddy yard. A mixture of horse manure and mud made walking carefully difficult. I slipped and slid, and by the time we approached the work area, my boots and trousers had a strong unpleasant smell about them.

"We will see the dressing floor first, Sir. The younger bal maidens do most of the work and good they are too."

We mounted an open floor, protected poorly from the elements by a rusting tin roof but no walls. To one side, several older girls with long-handled hammers broke ore into smaller pieces with a loud noise that shattered the ear.

All wore card gook hats that small ore chips, sent spitting wildly from the hammers, hit and pitted with such force.

"Them's spalling, Sir, and these girls"... he pointed to another group of four ..."are cobbing and crushing stones even smaller."

I watched with mounting concern as the young girls, some as young as ten years with the ragged dress, swung hammers, their breath misting as one in the cold air. My senses shocked, we moved quickly to the next dressing floor, the jigging house, where two lines of smaller girls stood either side of a large sieve sitting on top of a water tank. Their hands were red from the cold as they pushed the sieve back and forth with rhythm through running cold water. Some were in bare feet, and their dresses were soaked.

"They be lucky," said Pumblewood. "Three-pence a day. That be the same as the old men breaking fresh ore from the mine."

"But is there no warm, covered place for them? Is there nowhere to dry properly?"

"Nay, Sir, Silas Dench had none of that, despite your aunt's entreaties. She was a sharp pain in his side and glad he was when she passed."

I stood looking at the pathetic ragged figures, unable to imagine their discomfort and hardship. Angry and re-solved in mind, I turned on Pumblewood.

"We will see the mine, and I will climb down and visit the

men. And you, Sir, will tell me of my mother and aunt."

I waggled a finger under his nose and turned sharply away with clenched fists.

"Aye, Sir, but know you, the worst is yet to come," he mumbled.

We approached the mine. The adit, an entrance no taller than a stooped man and just wide enough for single file, laid before me pitch black and uninviting. Holding onto the roughhewn walls, we tripped and stumbled down the steep sloping passageway to the Devil's Hole, as Pumblewood called the vertical pit that was the center of all things. A continuous noise of picks breaking the seams and shovels loading ore into kibble skips echoed continually from far below us. This amid the hoarse cries of miners who worked the day breathing in and choking on thick dust; I felt we were entering hell itself.

Pumblewood, quiet since my remonstration, stopped and turned toward me with a candle in hand. The light showed a face that was troubled over a more serious matter than the terrible conditions around us.

His voice shook. "Dear Lord, Sir, this day has been coming, and still I am for the most part unable to satisfy your concerns."

"How so?" I asked. My concerns were mainly for my mother. Mr. Crumley gave the explanation to me that a skip full of ore had run amok as miners pulled it to the headframe wheel lift that hauled the ore up to the rail shaft. The skip ran over my mother. As no women worked below ground, the story made little sense.

"Silas Dench was a wicked man who would have his way in all things." Pumblewood put a handkerchief to his mouth and nose as a swirling mass of thick blinding dust carried on an updraft enveloped us. Coughing and spitting black phlegm on the ground, he continued. "I thought it strange that he should announce your mother's death to the workforce one morning. Not one of us was aware of the accident save two miners supposed involved, yet they agreed she died in the previous afternoon. Her body was already buried, and that was the end of things."

I kept my own counsel, wishing to think on Pumblewood's words. We reached a circular cavern and a narrow ledge that led around its entirety. Ladders leading down into the blackness leaned against wooden shoring on all sides. From one ladder, blackened faces silently looked in my direction as two men climbed to the ledge with boots and tools slung over shoulders.

"Your aunt also disappeared one night after a fight with Dench. She fought him tooth and nail and no mistake for better conditions for the workers."

"And she is buried with my mother?" I asked.

"It will be best you enquire with Mrs. Malocks," replied Pumblewood.

I sensed his guilty conscience and wondered if he and Mrs. Malocks were keepers of hurtful truth they preferred not to share.

We continued on the inspection, and later, as we cleaned ourselves in the office, I asked, "Can you show me where my mother is buried?"

Pumblewood sighed deeply and shook his head. "Dear Sir, I cannot. I fear no-one can."

"You and Mrs. Malock shall meet me in the kitchen to-morrow morning," I ordered sternly. I left him to ponder.

***

The warmth from the fire in my bedroom made my dressing habits more comfortable and my mind more ready for the day ahead. I had written to Mr. Crumley advising him that he take care of the mine's banking and see that I spent no more than one-quarter of the income on managing my personal affairs. Other requirements were to follow once I completed my inquiries into personal matters.

On hearing voices below, I knew that Pumblewood had arrived as requested and that, if my suspicions proved correct, he would hopefully, having the opportunity without my presence, be advising Mrs. Malocks that the truth about my mother and aunt should come to light. Without haste, I descended to the kitchen to find both my house-keeper and mine foreman drinking tea. I waved them remain seated as they made to stand.

Their conversation was finished as I entered and both

sat silent, each looking at the tea cup in front of them. I was determined to make sure both became aware of my intention to end their employment should they hold information back. It was Pumblewood who spoke.

"Your mother was sick," he said softly, "with the dust on her lungs."

As the sorrowful tale unfolded slowly, I learned of the cruel way my uncle caused my mother's untimely death by ignoring her. The thought of my mother suffering tore deeply at my heart. Sick with silicosis, more common known as black lung disease, and hardly able to walk, my mother came to the door asking Silas to fetch a doctor. He refused and sent her away. On the following morning, two miners found her at the bottom of the steep cliffs, pounded by the raging sea.

I looked into Malocks' face and saw a glistening. The burden of responsibility she shared with Pumblewood was too much. She burst into tears and buried her head in her hands, shaking her shoulders as if to lighten the load.

"Florence is buried near here," she sobbed uncontrollably.

It was the first time anyone spoke of my mother by name, and the mention stirred my emotions to the quick. Silas bribed the two men to bury her not two miles away in a pauper's cemetery. Even in death, she could find no dignity. It gave me no satisfaction that the man who abandoned her was also dead, for I wished him alive to face me on a day of reckoning.

My biggest shock was to come as I learned of my aunt. Malocks, too taken with her guilt to continue, prayed I would forgive her.

Pumblewood continued.

"Your aunt it was who carried on where your mother had finished. She fought almost every day with Silas, demanding better conditions for the hard-working women, especially the younger girls."

Silas had snapped and hurried to silence her. Within one week constables arrived to arrest her, declaring that her legal guardian certified her insane.

I could not imagine another act so evil and looked at Pumblewood with disgust. My fist crashed down onto the table, spilling the tea. Mrs. Malocks jumped and gave out a short scream.

"God help me," cried Pumblewood, "for it was I who helped him put her on the black coach."

Unable to control my emotions, I walked out and into the yard.

An hour later, since I stormed angrily from the kitchen, leaving Mrs. Malocks and Pumblewood guessing what fate I may have in store for them, I returned. Their disloyalty to the memory of my mother and aunt filled me with an incredible thirst to punish them. Yet, despite my misgivings, I was acutely aware that without their help the conclusion to my nightmare would forever leave unanswered questions and my mind in a state of turmoil. I had no reason to suppose that my aunt was alive, given the awful conditions within lunatic asylums. It remained for me to find her. The following morning I would set out for Scradsdale Asylum and determine my aunt's fate. But first I would visit my mother and speak with the local rector.

I returned to the kitchen. Pumblewood stood uneasily, shifting his weight from one foot to another. His eyes looked to the floor, and he clasped both hands in front of him. In silence, he waited at my pleasure as I instructed Mrs. Malocks to fetch her cloak and see me to the pauper's cemetery.

I turned to Pumblewood. "And you, Sir, will take up matters at the mine and we will speak of your right to continue there on my return."

Pumblewood looked up, his face broken with shame and guilt. "Yes, Sir," is all he replied before turning to make his leave.

A few moments later, accompanied by Mrs. Malocks, I rode to the cemetery to respect my mother, a poor body buried Beneath a wooden cross inscribed with the number three hundred and seventy-five. I stood looking at the grass-covered mound and the view through the waving tall storks and weeds at the sea in the distance. Row upon row of crosses, most weathered with age and broken, or split had fallen in amongst the long overgrown grass that now covered the entire field. Before leaving that cold and dreary place, I arranged with the rector to have my mother brought to Condurrow House for a fitting burial inside the grounds.

***

Scradsdale Asylum stood on top of a hill two miles inland and a mile away from the nearest hamlet. My disappointment at finding it closed and abandoned did not prevent me from walking in my aunt's fragile footsteps. One large rusted entrance gate swung lazily in the wind, screeching as it closed with a loud clang before blowing open again. Lichen covered the red brick walls that surrounded the overgrown garden, and the heavy smell of decaying nettles, Foxglove, and trailing Geraniums filled the air. The tall building itself, scarred with dozens of small barred windows, rose from the ground like an ugly Gothic creature emanating fear and dread of the unknown. The very sight of it made one shiver.

My feet crunched on broken glass as I entered this fearful place and a musty smell of decay in the still air made me choke. After I reached the first landing, I wondered at the row of iron doors and imagined from behind each one, a pathetic creature locked away in a permanent state of misery. The very walls, with peeling white paint, resounded with mad screams and whimperings of the lost and lonely souls who died within. Who can say if they were insane or not? For my aunt, it must have been a journey into Dante's hell.

Shaking, I was resolved to find her.

I left Scradsdale with darkened thoughts and journeyed all that day and into the night before reaching Truro and a comfortably furnished chamber. My mind was clearly set on meeting any doctor of note at Cornwall's largest hospital who might be able to help with directions to another asylum. With horse rested in White Horse coaching inn, I set out smartly in the carriage the following early morning. On reaching the imposing hospital, a clerk directed me to the office of one Doctor Jethro Tilling. An interesting man, I found the good doctor to be of wiry figure and tall; of old age and of smart appearance wearing black knee breeches and stockings, black morning coat and assisted in his walking with an elegant cane topped with a dragon's head of solid silver. He received me in a large office dominated by a rosewood desk adorned with scattered piles of books and an excellent brass microscope in pride of place on one corner of a display table.

I felt lulled of mind as I sat comfortably in the quiet surroundings. The soft ticking of the tall floor clock and the distant pitched screams of colorful peacocks parading the green around the building slowed the need to rush my day.

"You say your aunt was of sound mind," he commented as I finished my inquiry. He raised a finger and flicked his bottom lip up and down. "Of course she will in all probability be dead now after several years. The mad idiots live forever, and the sane die very quickly." His head shook vigorously. "Indeed they do, Sir, indeed they do."

I waited while he wrote on paper, the scratching quill nib rudely disturbing the quiet. On it, he wrote the whereabouts of the only other asylum, a place called Trelonwarren.

"Do not expect any miracles," he said as we parted. "If your aunt lives, she will in all probability be of dumb nature. Years without anyone sane to talk to will have silenced her tongue."

I shivered at the thought and bid the good doctor farewell.

***

A long waving row of bright Acer trees on either side of the drive leading to the main entrance gave the plain sandstone brick of Trelonwarren an air of importance. Behind the door, however, that importance vanished completely as I observed two attendants pushing a man roughly through a large wooden door into a hall. From within the hall the constant jabbering chatter, babbling, and screaming of the insane echoed off the high ceiling. The smell of sickness and sewer hung heavily in the air.

After speaking to the clerk, he instructed me to wait for the key warder, Mr. J. J. O'Brady, a man with knowledge of the inmates and places few of those who worked there ever visited. I shuddered and not for the first time. It was a morose feeling that chilled my spine.

"Well now, Mr. Jeddler," said O'Brady arriving, "a pleasure to be sure that I meet a real gentleman. Doctor Tilling sent you with note ... my ... my." He waved the note given to him by the clerk and held me with a sly look, his fat lips apart to reveal a large gap in his lower front teeth.

I took an instant dislike to him. He was grotesque in size with a pot belly and dressed in a worn green jacket and dirty white breeches. A tail of oily brown hair hung limply across his back, and a fat bare toe poked through one broken and scuffed shoe whose buckle had disappeared. His face bore signs of pox, scars from boils, and a weeping spot that looked picked. He held the note with dirty fingers and, bending slightly, passed wind. A more rude and shameless man I had never met.

He shook a ring of keys before me. "Mr. Jingle Jangle they call me. Shall we go find your mad aunt?"

"She is here then," I exclaimed.

He laughed. "Yes, in the pit."

O'Brady led me along a passage and down some stone steps, his unmelodic whistling adding to the somewhat violent but melancholy atmosphere of the place. He swung his lantern back and forth as he waddled in front of me. This served to encourage our shadows to dance back and forth on the bare brick wall that glistened with damp and smelled of mildew. And all the while the all-pervasive stench of humanity affected me greatly. I took a kerchief from my pocket and covered my nose.

Apart from the lantern, the only illumination at the bottom of the stairs came from narrow shafts of light emanating from barred windows that stood at ground level along the back of the asylum. Each window looked down into a gloomy cellar dungeon, closed to the passage by a rusted iron bar grid and a locked door.

O'Brady turned to me and sniggered, his fat, unshaven face grotesque in the lantern's glow.

"These mad ones are lucky Mr. Jeddler; they all have a chamber of their own." He laughed loudly and kicked the nearest door. "Wake up mad woman, there's a gentleman comes a-callin' for you."

With apprehension, I stepped toward the bars and peered into the cell. Taking the lantern, I raised it high so as to see much of the cell and the wretch within it. What nightmarish apparition appeared before my eyes would I never forget as long as I lived. My aunt, for I assumed her to be so, lay sprawled about on the dirty tiled floor like a bundle of rags. As she raised her head of long unkempt silver hair, I looked into her eyes and recoiled with horror. Her mouth moved as though forming words but none reached my ears; her eyes seeing but not seeing me.

"I will have her out of this vile place this very day," I said angrily, grabbing O'Brady by his coat.

O'Brady grinned. "Two pounds, Sir. She's nearly done for, and no-one here will care. One less mouth to feed and one less grave."

With trembling hand, for I sorely refrained from giving vent to my feelings and thrashing the man, I paid the scoundrel and bid him order me a coach and four for a trip back to Condurrow.

***

Two hours later after wrapping my aunt in a warm woolen cloak, I helped her into the carriage and sat with an arm about her shoulder. Such a sorry sight she was that I fought tears and anger in equal amount. That such a frail and innocent lady be treated so cruelly was beyond my understanding.

As we traveled, she said nothing nor looked at anything, her eyes staring ahead. I hoped that her new surroundings might in time bring her back to her senses and learn I was her nephew.

At last, as Condurrow House came into view, I saw the front door open and Mrs. Malocks descending the steps to the drive. As I journeyed, I was aware that a nurse would be appropriate for my aunt's needs and Mrs. Malocks could not do two jobs. I would find a girl from the village.

The coach stopped and as the door opened my aunt looked upon Mrs. Malocks and let out a scream so frightening before having a feint. I carried my aunt into the house and laid her upon a couch in front of the fire Malocks had set upon my instructions.

"Tis my punishment and salvation," cried Mrs. Malocks, "to welcome home this poor soul. May God help us both."

"Indeed, I said. "God is the only one who can forgive you for I do not believe I ever will."

Malocks hurried back to the kitchen to fetch tea, still crying.

***

Two days later, my mother returned, her black carriage looked upon by the respectful miners and their families as it made its way slowly to Condurrow from the pauper's field.

A silence descended upon our small group of mourners as my mother's remains arrived. The undertaker Mr. John Nathidius, in respectful regalia, walked with a steady, measured step at the head of the sad cortège. In his right hand he carried a swagger cane which, with practiced ceremony, he raised a little with each step and flicked sharply to the right and then back again after tapping the ground. Behind him four black horses dressed with plumed feathers nodded in time, their hooves crunching on the gravel as they pulled the glass-sided carriage. Behind, I followed in a small procession with four women from the village, hired to help mourn my loss. Their practiced wailing did much to make a sad occasion.

Mr. Crumley had arrived the previous day. His insistence on attending the funeral filled me with some cheer as I wished to speak with him on mining matters. He stood waiting with Mrs. Malocks and Captain Pumblewood on the steps of the house, hat in hand. Up above them, looking down upon us from a window was my aunt, still silent and forlorn in a world of her mind's making. As the cortège made its way to the garden, the small group walked slowly with us. With due respect, my mother was laid to rest. As the gravediggers went about their task afterwards, we made our way to the reception.

"I would speak with you on a matter of urgency," whispered Mr. Nathidius as I paid his fee.

Our company sat in the drawing room around a dining table filled with a variety of refreshments and hot tea. Most joined in the quiet conversation. I ushered Mr. Nathidius into the hall and waited for him to pocket his fee. Stooped at the shoulders, and with thin face together with a hooked nose, he displayed an appearance I feared might frighten a child.

"I found this buried with your mother and thought you might wish to speak with the Sheriff and his constables."

He produced a rusting hammer head from his pocket; a bal maiden's spalling hammer.

"Why would I wish to speak with the Sheriff?" I asked.

Nathidius bowed his head. "Not wishing to sadden or annoy you any further, I am bound to tell you that this I found inside your mother's skull."

***

On the morning after discussing business with Mr. Crumley and seeing him off at the station, I rode back to Condurrow House deep in thought. I said nothing to Crumley, or indeed discussed the matter with anyone.

My first thought was of Silas Dench who, in my opinion, was wicked enough to attack a woman. Two men buried her, but I was sure they would have seen the hammer although Nathidius did say the hammer was inside her skull. Anger welled up within me for I was aware that without a telling clue or confession I may never find the solution.

It was in my mind to question Pumblewood and Malocks, but I was fearful that if they played a part in a murder, they might vanish. Far better, I thought, to look into the affair a little closer and then call the Sheriff.

I tapped on the carriage wall behind the coachman and called for him to let me off at the cliff path leading down to the mine.

After a short walk, I came to the cleared yard and the engine house. A gaggle of bal maids stood with hands on hips, watching me approach.

"Respects to your mother, Sir," said one. "We would be

speaking to you if you have a mind to listen to how she died. We knows what happened.

The woman with a weather-beaten face and squinting blue eyes, standing rigidly with folded arms and tight lips, looked at me suspiciously from beneath her gook hat.

I could feel her deep mistrust of me and with good reason. Silas Dench left not a brass farthing for their meager upkeep and with coldest damp weather upon us, my responsibilies weighed heavily upon me. Without wages, most of the men were finding work elsewhere while the women continued to work every day on the dwindling stock of ore under Pumblewood's supervision. All hoped for recompense for some two months' hard work.

"Tell me," I asked calmly, for I did not wish to test the woman's patience. "What is it you know?"

"I see the devil, that Dench, come to your mother's house and drag her screaming into a pony and trap. It was him and the woman what took her, Sir. She were in no mine fall nor any bad state of twisted mind to do her life away."

I was thoroughly convinced from the woman's agitated state and the other bal maidens' nodding heads that the account she gave was one they all honestly believed was the truth of the tragic matter. After thanking them and assuring them money I received from the bank that very afternoon was going to reach their empty pockets, my heart lifted to see them smile.

My mind, however, was on other more pressing matters.

***

The sheriff resided comfortably in one small room at the village Anchor Inn and was greedily eating crusted pork pie when I arrived. Of mature years, Septimus Beatocks was a man no-one would argue with unless of a stronger will. A heavily built man with much muscle, he towered over me. His lined face, with an unshaven chin, showed much sign of firm resolve while dark brown unblinking eyes pierced the very heart and soul out of those who dared tell an untruth. His loose, silvery black hair hung unfastened about his broad shoulders, giving him an unkempt appearance. Yet his dress suggested a caring wife allowing order to his busy life. Pressed were his trousers below a frock coat that when fully opened revealed a buttoned waistcoat of dark blue.

He puffed his red cheeks and continually pushed his fat bottom lip forward as I told him of my discovery and my thinking on the matter. There could only have been one woman with Silas Dench on that fateful night. Spurned by my uncle, Mrs Malocks still hid a secret love in her heart and would doubtless, in her misguided mind, blindly do the man's bidding.

"I think you have made a good point, Mr. Jeddler, and no mistake," said Septimus. "And where is Mrs. Malocks at this moment?"

Fear caused me to weaken at the knees, for I had clearly not given more thought to the imminent danger that my aunt faced back at Condurrow House.

"Alone with my aunt," I replied, springing to my feet.

"Then we be away, Sir, and quick about it. Pray God we are in time to save your aunt from any harm and arrest Malocks." He strode quickly ahead of me to the courtyard. "If you are right, Sir," he said over his shoulder, "the gallows be awaiting to serve justice."

Minutes later both of us galloped ahead of the constable's black carriage. What awaited us as the house came into view filled me with anguish. My aunt stood unsteadily on the steps, a spalling hammer in her hands. Of Mrs. Malocks there was no sign.

Beatocks took the hammer from my aunt and gave it a thorough examination. Satisfied that no blood stained the head of the tool, he ordered a constable to accompany my aunt to the living room while he and I searched the house for Mrs. Malocks. It was with some relief that we found the house unoccupied for I feared the worst. It looked as though the woman had absconded, fearful for her life, although I was mystified as to how she would know I visited the sheriff.

"There be something not right, but without Malocks' presence we must wait awhile," declared Beatocks. "The hammer came from the mine though not carried here by your aunt."

A little while later, as he mounted his horse, a constable came running from the direction of the cliff edge. Short of breath and red in the face, he exclaimed that a body lay at the foot of the cliff. With haste, we ran to the path and made our way down past the mine and through the surf to a small area of shingle and scattered rocks. Malocks lay face down, her broken body arched in a grotesque form. Blood covered her head, matting her hair. "She took her own life, I declare," said Beatocks. "Your aunt would not have strength enough to push another in a struggle."

I kept my own counsel for my senses told me all was not as simple as Beatocks suggested.

With the body removed by the constables and the Sheriff taking his leave, I hurried to my aunt's side after summoning a woman from the mine to comfort her.

***

It was the next morning after Malocks' death when the most disturbing occurrence forced me to make a decision that I still ponder might have changed my life and reputation forever.

I had disposed of my shirt and breeches and other grubby clothing into the laundry basket and discovered a worrisome sight 'neath some sheets. A small apron frilled about the edge lay rolled into a ball. A smudge of blood attracted my attention, and I unrolled the cloth. To my horror,

I found much staining in such a manner that suggested the apron wiped something clean. The apron belonged to my aunt, and I spent a sleepless night tossing and turning. Should I tell the sheriff? Did someone else bring the hammer to my aunt or did that person kill Malocks and leave the hammer that my aunt may have found and wiped with innocence? As dawn broke that morning I decided to say nothing; not a word to anyone for fear of opening a wound that would affect many.

And so I choose to believe that whatever happened, justice smiled for my mother and aunt; something more precious than the secret my conscience spent little time contemplating.

**

It was the spring some months later when I looked upon the newly repaired engine house and enclosed jigging floor. My inheritance, all but spent on repairs, renewed the vigor and gratitude of the workers. A new shaft that promised much tin produced more and more ore each day, mined by men with an extra tuppence a day in pocket and supervised by a much reformed Captain Pumblewood. All was well including my renewed and, I must say, welcoming admittance back into the Amalgamated Tin Mine Association by Edwin Malby, the Chairman. Indeed, the gentleman visited me on some occasions and much it was

I learned from his experience in the industry.

Of my aunt, I feared she would not talk again, but her recovery was such that she enjoyed the garden and carriage rides to market. Her life was improved, and many hours she sat with the new housekeeper playing cards or reading. Life was indeed idyllic save the secret I chose to keep within my conscience.

Captain Pumblewood stood with me on the cliff, surveying the mine below and listening to the noise from the jigging house.

"That be the most wonderful sound," he said, grinning.

"And what would that be, Pumblewood?" I asked.

He put a hand to one ear as though to hear more clearly. "Why, Sir, that be the sweet, happy sound of a bal maid a knocking ore at Condorrow Mine."

57

STARTING OVER

Although a tale for young adults, this story has its roots in incidents related over many years regarding alien abduction. Who's to say these reports are not accurate?

I believe ... do you?

"No," insisted Benjamin. "There was no wind, and I've seen that funny face before on 'The X-Files' – the one looking down the well ...."

Mom passed years earlier, and Pop tried to run our small orchard farm, but the bank was repossessing. Hank, that's my brother, left before that happened, promising to keep in touch but he never did. I got a couple of letters, but nothing else. Hank had seen the end coming and urged Pop to move into a retirement home. There was dough under the floorboards, so to speak, but Pop wouldn't have it, saying he'd rather die on his own sod than someone else's.

That was Pop. Stubborn to the end.

Last month, he had a stroke. After the ambulance left, something told me he wasn't coming back.

I called Hank right away and spoke to him for a minute, telling him I was on the way to join him after dealing with dad – then I lost him – I mean, his voice just faded and, like, it seemed someone just cut the whole cell system to hell. Mad at not getting on with telling him dad was in the hospital, I decided that as soon as possible I'd drive down to Jacksonville from my hometown, Homerville, a small place on the edge of the Okefenokee Swamp. I guess what I really wanted was an excuse to get away from Georgia and head for the good times Hank kept telling me about. Florida was where the dollar was at, and he was already earning. I planned to take a short flight from Jacksonville, dumping the old Dodge pick-up at the airport.

A few days later, I finished packing and was down in the basement when it happened. There was a distant rumble, and within a second or two the house shook. It rocked a second time, then everything went so quiet I could hear my own breathing. My first reaction was – twister. I crawled under a workbench, and that was all I remembered until I woke with the sun in my eyes. The house was gone, a mangled mess of splintered black smoking wood and glass. From where I lay, I could see our tractor, upside down on the road at the bottom of the drive. Power lines were down, and a few of the poles leaned at different crazy angles.

Blood oozed out of a couple of cuts but other than some bruises, that was it. I looked at my watch and was amazed. I'd been unconscious for twelve hours. My biggest shock came when I managed to climb out of the basement. As far as the horizon, all the fields and trees were black and smoldering. I didn't waste any time. Help would probably take a few days if I was lucky and anyway, I was already joining Hank. I got my stuff together, or what there was left of it, and after cleaning my cuts I headed down the road.

***

It took two days to reach the State line and two more to reach the outskirts of Jacksonville. More specifically, I was headed for International Drive, Orlando, the last place I heard from my brother Hank before all this crap hit the fan. I remember him telling me a real big storm was brewing and the sky there was turning black as we spoke. His was the last voice I heard - apart from the one recounting memories in my head.

I sat and cried when it hit me a day later. Three miles out of Jacksonville and the black horizon was still there as I rested for the night. The following morning was when I saw green in the distance intermingled with piles of wood and brick where homes and shops used to be. Hell, man, it was like I was living in some kind of nightmare. There were loads of friggin' destruction, and you'd think there'd be bodies, but there wasn't a one. That made me feel there'd been a mass evacuation of some kind to Jacksonville.

The highway into town was strewn with cars and trucks, and I kept hoping to see someone as I got to the outskirts.

"You've got to eat, Ray," I shouted out loud.

That's a real funny feeling – shouting and listening to your own voice, the only voice you've heard in days. I don't know why I shouted, but it felt good. Maybe I was getting tired of the silence. Jeez, not even a bird had so much as squawked. The sky was empty, and I thought about 9/11. Without meeting anyone, it was hard to know what the heck had happened. It sure wasn't a twister, that was for certain.

"Gypsy, wish you were along on this one, boy," I said wistfully.

Gypsy, my hound dog, had died the previous year of old age I guessed. He was great at tracking and sniffing out anything that wriggled in the grass. Pop got him for me on my fifteenth birthday, and from then on, me and Gypsy went everywhere together. I trained him proper, but Pop said the dog was really training me. That's what the old man was good at. He never let me get a swollen head and told me: "You look after that hound dog, and he'll be your buddy for life, never asking too much of you except your undying love." And so it proved to be because me and Gypsy ate and slept together. I missed him.

Damn near got all sad at that thought and decided to

think about getting something to eat. I hadn't thought to bring any food with me except some cookies and soda.

Jacksonville was wasted. There wasn't a soul or animal around. Behind what used to be an apartment block, I found a supermarket, half of it still standing. I spent some time climbing over the stuff scattered all over the floor and filled a trolley with mainly cans and coffee and the like. I guessed no-one was going to miss it. I sat on a checkout stool later and opened a can of peaches. They tasted great.

"Come on out and talk to me," I called. "Even if you're a zombie, get the hell out here."

That made me laugh. I thought about all those zombie movies Gypsy and me used to watch on TV. I looked around the store and found a burner for a fondue set and lit it so I could brew some coffee.

"Howzabout a coffee, pal?" I asked an imaginary friend.

That's when I started to cry. I guess I was scared of being on my own. I started thinking that maybe everyone was dead and I was like the Omega man, the one in that movie. I even thought there might be some zombies around but knew there weren't really. I just didn't like being on my own

My Pop used to say that you never really miss anyone or anything until they're gone. I guess that's what hit me the most after several days on the road.

I decided to make for Saint Augustine, a small town over on the coast, taking with me as many supplies as I could.

My hunting rifle and plenty of ammo were top of the list. I remembered what happened when Katrina hit and all those news pictures on TV showing the looters and such. I could do without any of that – that's if there was anyone else around.

I picked up a few small tools and then the biggest back-pack I could find in the store. I figured water and tin food I could get along the way. After stuffing the pack full, I settled down for the night, still trying to figure out what the hell had happened.

In my heart, I knew Hank wouldn't be in Orlando. Bigger and stronger than me, he'd do the same as me if he was alive – head for the coast.

I planned on getting a small cruiser, not that I ever had one, but I was good with engines and reckoned I could handle the boat as long as I stayed near the coast. Miami was the best place to head. Mind you, Miami was a long way to go. That's where people would be if there were any left alive though.

I was beginning to think like a survivor, I suppose. I had to look after myself.

"Hey, Mister."

It was getting dark, and I was real tired. My head was playing tricks with me.

"Hey, Mister."

I sat bolt upright. It was a kid's voice. I waited.

"Hey, Mister, I seen ya. Can I sleep with you?"

The kid sounded real sad, but I wasn't gonna get caught with my pants down, so to speak.

I picked up my rifle. "Over here, kid. Take it easy. I got a gun."

Tin cans and packets of whatever fell or rolled noisily as the kid approached me. He appeared from around a freezer and stood looking at me. He was black and was smaller than me.

"What's your name?" I asked.

"Benjamin." He stared at me and the rifle wide-eyed for some time. "I don't have a gun, mister, honest."

I didn't know whether to laugh or cry. Meeting someone I could talk to was like receiving a birthday present.

He came over and sat next to me, and I judged him around nine or ten. Long streaky hair ran down his back, and a Cardinals T-shirt covered the top of a worn pair of jeans.

"Well, Benjamin, my name is Ray."

"So where you headed, Ray? Can I come along?"

"Sure, why not. I wanna get a boat at Saint Augustine and head south – see what I can find."

"We might be safe from them there," he murmured.

"Safe – from who? What happened?"

Benjamin was leaning against my shoulder, fast asleep.

I didn't get much sleep myself, even though I'd not slept much since everyone went missing. I kept thinking about what Benjamin had said – about us being safe from them.

Who he was talking about was a mystery. I wanted to shake him awake to find out, but he needed to sleep too, so I just sat and thought. Maybe it was something to do with a nuclear war. That was something Pop always warned me about. "Never trust the darned Reds," he'd say.

It got light around five, and a few minutes later Benjamin woke and yawned. I got up and made us some coffee, and we had cereals with some milk that was still cold in the big fridge.

"So who are we safe from when we get to Miami?" I asked. "Has there been a war or did someone invade us?"

Benjamin stopped eating, milk dribbling down his chin. "You don't know a lot, do you?" He stuffed a spoonful of cornflakes into his mouth. "Did you hide when it happened?"

I told him I didn't remember. When the storm hit, I was knocked out and didn't wake up until the next day.

"So who are they and what happened to you? Why didn't you disappear?"

"I was cleaning the leaves out of the well, and my brother Tim wouldn't pull me back up, and that's how I saw them."

"So you saw something down the well?"

"No!"

Benjamin stopped eating and started to cry. I wanted to understand. I put an arm around his shoulder.

"Tim and my mom have gone, and I don't know where to find them, and you've got to help me."

He wiped his nose and looked at me.

"Okay," I said. "Tell me what happened from when you got up."

Benjamin's chest heaved with a big sigh. "Mom told me to clean the leaves out of the well on our farm and Tim was to lower me on the bucket. When the leaves are in the bucket, he pulls me up again. Then we have breakfast. But when I shouted for him, he wasn't there, and this funny face looked down at me and started pulling me up. I got scared and screamed, and he let me go. Then the big black cloud came over, and everything went dark."

"What happened then?"

"Nothing," sobbed Benjamin. "I climbed up the rope and Mom, and Tim had gone."

"So what did you find when you climbed out of the well, apart from Mom and Tim missing?"

"The house was smashed on the ground. Even old Foggy, our laborer, had gone, but his tractor engine was still running."

"I think there was a few twisters, Benjamin. Nothing else can do all that."

"No," insisted Benjamin. "There was no wind, and I've seen that funny face before on 'The X-Files' – the one looking down the well."

I wanted to laugh but decided to keep him happy. What happened was a big mystery, but funny creatures or monsters was too silly.

We finished a packet of chocolate biscuits and downed a last cup of coffee before packing more stuff into a backpack I found at the rear of the store. All the time we were getting ready I kept thinking about Benjamin's insistence there was no wind. If there was no wind, then something must have pushed buildings over – but what? The biggest mystery was where the heck had all the people gone? It beat me, but I knew I'd find out sooner or later.

My brother, Hank, said that to me once after he found me dazed on the ground after I fell out of a tree. I wasn't supposed to climb trees due to me bein' four years old, so I lied and said I just tripped. Later, my mom told me off while we were having dinner for losing a shoe, but Hank laughed and produced my shoe from under the table. He found it in the crook of two branches up the tree where it got stuck. He grinned and said, "I knew I'd find out sooner or later."

Benjamin ended my thinking.

"I'm just about ready," he puffed, pushing a trolley in front of him.

He took the backpack from me and slung it over his shoulder. For someone his age, he sure was tough.

"I reckon we could fill this with water bottle packs and get ourselves a truck or car. That way we can carry all we need. Right?"

We high-fived, and he winked. "You can call me Ben if you like."

I did like that. Ben was a nice kid, and I kind of took to him. He was no mommy's boy, and it was obvious he was used to work.

"Okay," I agreed. "Let's see if we can find us a Caddie."

"Don't matter if there's no keys," said Ben. "I can hot-wire any darned set of wheels."

We pushed the trolley out of the store and started down the road. There was no Caddie, but there was a new GMC three-quarter ton with plenty of fuel. Loaded up, we hit the road although Ben couldn't see much. His red Cardinal's baseball cap just about popped above the dash.

There were a couple of service areas on the highway, and each one became a rest stop for us. Huge eighteen wheelers, trucks, and cars littering the highway meant we had to keep slowing down as we weaved in and out amongst them.

As it grew dark, I suggested we stop for the night at the next place we came to; perhaps a motel 6.

Then the strangest of things happened. Our truck just died on us. I twisted the key, but nothing happened, and that's when Ben screamed.

The sky turned black, and a blinding shaft of light hit us.

"They found us. They're here. I told you they'd find us."

"Who, for cryin' out loud."

I heard Ben shout like he was out of the truck; off in the distance.

Then I saw it. Staring through the windshield.

It was tall and had long arms, but I couldn't see much else as the light was coming from behind. I was shaking, trying to make sense of everything. Then two big yellow eyes came close to the screen. A long tongue with frothy stuff on it slapped the screen leaving a trail of dribble running down to the hood.

I wanted to run but couldn't. I was holding my breath and then screamed as loud as I could. I jerked my head sideways, but Ben had gone. The strange thing was, his door was shut, and I knew it was locked. I always flicked the central lock when I got into a truck. Pop had been in an accident once and spent time in hospital because he fell out of a truck after not closing the door right. That's how I knew. So it was weird that Ben got out.

The bright light faded and I could see the trees either side of the highway. The truck's headlights were dead, and the starter motor didn't even click when I tried turning the engine again. Scared, I looked through the screen, but whatever it was out there had gone. All I could see was a clear road.

I began to calm down, and without thinking, I unlocked and opened my door. Ben couldn't be far away.

I guess that was the most stupid thing I ever did.

"Ben," I shouted. "Come on, it's gone. Let's go."

There was a loud click right behind me as someone readied an automatic – a noise I knew well as Hank, my brother, used to have one.

"Okay, take it real easy and put both hands up in the air."

I nearly fainted with relief. It's the army, I thought. I must have seen things, and Ben musta got to me. Boy, was I gonna give him hell when I caught up with him.

"It's okay mister, I'm with my friend, and we're just trying to get to Miami. Say, can you tell me what happened? I came to after the storm, and everyone's disappeared."

He didn't answer me, and then I heard him talking.

"Yeah, we got another one. I'm afraid we lost his partner. We got here too late. Yeah – I'll bring him in."

I turned to the soldier in time to see a strange small craft, lit up, come down the road, flying a few feet above the ground. It was the size of a car and stopped above us before lowering to the tarmac.

"Cool. How long have you had these? I bet they're top secret, right?"

The side of the craft slid back. I reckoned these guys were Special Forces or something like that. I didn't recognize the dark green uniform. The other soldier sat next to me, and the craft rose slowly. As we reached treetop level, we took off fast.

"Can you tell me …"

"Our boss will explain everything to you," said the driver.

"But we have to find Ben."

"Fraid he's gone, son. They've got him."

So Ben was right. There were monsters, and who were these guys?"

I was pushed back into my seat as the craft's nose tilted up and a glowing blue light surrounded us. I gripped the sides of my chair as the last thing I saw was the tops of the trees.

***

"He's awake."

I heard the voice as my eyes slowly opened. All I could see was a strange long white face and two huge scary orange flecked eyes. My legs and arms were strapped to a table. Around me everything was white. A bright light shone down on me. My chest thumped. I was so scared, it was hard to talk. "Hello." I tried to sound normal, but I was trying hard not to cry.

"I'm Kraal," said the white face.

He took a step back so I could see him better. He was tall and thin and dressed in a one piece white suit.

"I expect you're wondering where you are."

His long bony fingers touched my arm, and I tried to shrink back. "What's going on, mister?" I asked.

"You are one of the lucky ones," he answered. "Our force is saving whoever we can find alive before we finish the Drunagors for good. We cannot do this until we are sure the last survivors are rescued."

I looked confused as he untied the straps holding me to the table.

"Let me explain," he said.

I sat up and turned, sitting on the edge of the table. We were in a large room with curved walls, but there was no other furniture except another table with surgical tools and some equipment standing nearby. Behind it, two more white-faced people sat behind a window, looking at me.

"Many millenniums from now, Earth will be part of a Confederation of fifty worlds – planets, you call them. One of these worlds, Druna, will spend years building a fleet of warships which they will use to try to conquer the Confederation. Their ultimate goal is to control water supplies that are shipped out from ten of the worlds, Earth being one of them. Astro Command and the Confederation cannot allow that to happen. It would mean the end of everything we have achieved to create a peaceful existence between our governments."

I felt I was in some kind of a dream. I knew I wasn't as soon as Kraal touched me. "So what happened to all the people on Earth?"

"Vaporized. We are sorry, Ray but they felt nothing. Some, like you, survived. Now Drunagors are trying to kill off any survivors, and we have several ships around Earth trying to save them, mainly the young."

"So you're from the future?"

"Yes, and what has happened took place many years before the Confederation was formed. The Drunagors conquered here swiftly as you know and made Earth part of their empire. It was only recently that we perfected the ability to travel back so far. Now we can change the course of history and defeat our enemy before forming the Confederation."

I scratched my arm.

"It will stop itching soon." Kraal said.

He pointed to a small red mark on my skin. "That chip will record your medical condition and location."

I looked confused.

"You have the right temperament and courage. We are sending you back to help find survivors, including Ben."

I didn't understand too much but knew I was on the right side of a war from the future. It was hard to understand how I was involved and how things had happened, but I did want to rescue Ben, the only friend I had.

I jumped off the table and together with Kraal, boarded a small floating platform that arrived outside in the passage.

It was annoying that I didn't get a chance to explore. I mean, I was in a real spaceship and being sent back before meeting the Captain. These guys from the future were trying to stop the bad guys in the past from taking over the Earth and causing trouble. Damn, it was a lot to try and get my head around and really, I was a bit worried. If the bad guys, these Drunagors, could be wasted, then I guess those of us left would be starting over again. That'd be a real big job, but at least for now I had a few more friends.

Krall, I found out, was from another planet, Onger, and a

Confederation member, working with Astro Command as a medic alongside Jed and Zaren, one of the search crews who saved me.

All this was racing around in my head as we whizzed along a long curved wide passage. We transferred to the hover vehicle used when I got picked up. We stopped in front of a large door, and the hood of our transport slid forward, closing us in. The door opened, and we floated into a chamber marked 'AIRLOCK.' As soon as the door closed behind, another in front of us opened, and all I remember was a ring of blue light surrounding us again.

***

It was daylight as we lowered slowly to the road where I lost Ben. The truck was still there, but the rest of the road was deserted.

Jed, the pilot, turned to Zaren. "Run through the instructions on the Decib Meter again."

Zaren was teaching me to use a detector and a gun that zapped the Drunagors

The detector, a tablet with a push button control set and speaker, detected voices up to two krints away, about a mile in old measurement according to Zaren.

"Remember," said Zaren, "if all you hear is grunting or a kind of loud clucking, that'll be a Drunagor. Have the gun ready in case you come across a Drunagor or are attacked.

They have to touch and hold you for several seconds before you vaporize so don't hesitate. Just shoot them with your Disintegrator first."

He sounded like Pop. I remember Pop tellin' me on my first deer hunt: "Don't hesitate, son. As soon as you have him fair in them thar sights you pull the darn trigger while holdin' yer breath."

After setting down on the road, I got out with the equipment and strapped the gun to my back.

We spread out, and I moved into the woods with the meter switched on. My Disintegrator was gripped firmly in my other hand. I was freakin' scared and shakin', but I wasn't going to let Ben down. I knew he was out there.

I hadn't walked far when I heard a loud clucking and twigs snapping nearby. I stopped, my hands shaking. It was a Druganor – it had to be. My tablet dropped to the floor, and I swung around to where the noise came from.

As I did, a large claw-like grey hand grip my shoulder. Something wet dribbled on my ear as hot breath blew down my neck.

I gulped with fright and raised my Disintegrator, firing nervously and hitting his leg. His yellow eyes closed and an enormous brown tongue shot from his mouth, accompanied by a long high-pitched howl that echoed through the trees. Long teeth protruded from behind curled lips. His claw slid from my shoulder and he dropped to the ground. In seconds, there was nothing except a gooey red and green gel that smelled like our old cattle-shed back home.

"Hey, you okay?"

Jed crashed through the undergrowth and put a hand over his mouth. "They smell as bad as they look."

I picked up my Decib Meter and followed him.

Then something weird happened. I heard a shout coming from some way off. Still scared and nervous, the shout sounded familiar as I stumbled along. Jed kept going.

I tried to keep up, but he was in some kind of hurry.

"I just got a message from control. Seems like the Druganor's are losing too many men. Some of their ships have moved out. This could be the start of the end and victory for the Federation."

It was then I tripped over a fallen branch and crashed to the ground. Jed turned and almost screamed.

"Stop! We're friends."

With a large piece of the branch in his hands, held above his head, and ready to strike, was Ben. Behind him stood two other kids.

"Jeeze, Ray, I thought you were a monster. You okay? Who's that drifter with ya?"

I laughed. "This ain't no drifter, Ben. He's helping save us. He's from another world of the future. Kinda like them X Files movies only he's for real."

Ben looked serious and then, very slowly, his grubby face creased into a smile. "Yeah, right."

I quickly gave him the lowdown on my abduction and how we could be taken back to a new future world.

"No way," scowled Ben. "We're making it to Miami like you planned. We can survive there."

"Most of the survivors are going," I said. "If we stay, things will be tough. There will be a few Druganors to fight."

Jed tossed me another disintegrator and a tablet.

"You'll need this, Ray." He winked. He knew I'd stay.

"I've got to go. I wish you guys all the best." With that, he disappeared into the trees.

I turned to Ben and the boys. "We should get onto the highway to avoid skirmishes. We'll camp for the night in the central median and get some sleep. Tomorrow will be the start of a long trip."

"Was Jed a spaceman?" asked Drew, Ben's friend.

"Yes, he was, and they came to stop something that affected the future. It was the Druganors who caused all the fires and killed people because they wanted to rule a Druganor world. Jed and the Federation rescued many and are taking them to a safe haven in the future."

The boy looked terrified.

That night, I kept one eye open and a hand on my gun.

Dawn came around five the next morning. It was the usual time to rise at home. Pop would be in the kitchen beating eggs and frying bacon. My brother would be drinking black coffee and watching the news. I guess we got so used to an early rise when the farm was running well, and no matter what, we carried on as usual even though there weren't that much to do.

I lit our small primus stove and poured water in a small saucepan. We had plenty of coffee. Pop always said that even if there were no darn eggs to chew on, it was import-ant to drink coffee. It woke you up and got your pipes work-ing. He had some funny sayings, but they all made sense.

"You makin' coffee?"

Ben climbed out of his sleeping bag and slid on his ass down the wet bank to where I was at.

"I've got some granola bars," he said. He held a couple up in triumph. "I got enough for all of us."

"Tell me," I asked. "What happened to you in the truck that night? The door and window were still closed after you left."

Ben scowled. "That thing pulled the door open, grabbed me, and then closed it again while the light was blindin' you. I shouted and managed to wriggle free. I ran and met up with Drew and Vincent. Last thing I saw was the monster looking down the road and disappearin' into the trees."

His face dropped. "I was scared, Ray. I've been lookin' for you ever since though, honest."

The water began to boil.

"I know, Ben. I was lookin' for you too." I nudged him and pointed up the slope of grass. "Why not go get them up, Lieutenant? Let's have coffee and a bite. Nothing like startin' out early."

Ben grinned broadly and gave me a mock salute. "Okay Cap."

We drank our fill and loaded up. I decided that as long as possible, we should keep to the central meridian of highways, so we had a clear view for quite a way on all sides. We had two Disintegrators and a Decib meter along with a real shotgun that Vincent had got from a gun store.

I felt safe and made us walk in single file. "We should imagine we're huntin' deer," I said. "Keep quiet and move with eyes lookin' everywhere."

It was a few hours later that Drew screamed. "It's them – over there!" He screamed again and pointed behind us.

We all screamed. From the trees on one side came dozens of the tall creatures. They were clucking and bent over, looking at us with yellow eyes. Some had their long brown tongues flopping about as they ran toward us.

I shivered, dropped my gun and backpack.

"Run!" I shouted.

I tripped as the first creature reached out to grab me.

***

A sharp pain shot through my head and I could hear voices in the background. They kind of echoed softly but you could tell they were shouting. Then it was one voice. It was a voice I recognized, Hank, my brother. Confused, I wondered where he had come from. As I got to my feet, a hand grabbed my shoulder. With a loud shout, I reached for the Disintegrator but picked up a piece of wood instead.

"What in hell's name is goin' on with you, boy?"

Hank looked real concerned at me as I threatened him with the lump of a chair leg.

We were standing in the basement surrounded by broken shelves, furniture and an enormous jumbled pile of tools and fixings laying on the floor.

I scratched my head, trying to understand why I was back home.

"I come back for you when Pop died, and I was just in time to catch the storm and hid under my truck. I watched the house get torn apart and hoped you were okay. Thank the Lord you are. You must have been knocked out."

"How many days ago was that?" I asked.

Hank grinned. "Boy, you sure are out of it, ain't ya? The storm passed over 'bout an hour ago, that's all."

I started shaking my head. "No, that's wrong. It had to be at least three, maybe four days." I recounted what had happened and how I had met the two agents from the Federation. Heck, I told him everything and all he kept doing was laughing.

He hauled me out of the wreck that was our home and up on the road. As far as the eye could see there were fields of corn and some grazin' land. There weren't nothing burnt.

"I don't understand," I said. "I was a few miles away

outside Jackson."

"You been watchin' too many sci-fi movies and the like. C'mon, let's get some stuff together and get back to Miami. I got a good job there and an apartment for us."

"But Hank, I'm trying to explain. The world was nearly taken over by aliens, and me and my friends helped the Federation..."

"Stop." Hank held a hand up. "I don't want to hear another word about the aliens. They don't exist. It's all in your imagination."

For the next hour, we packed a lot of belongings into Hank's truck, and I kept thinking of ways I could prove what had really happened. I knew we had been abducted, but I needed the Disintegrator or the Decib Meter or no one would believe me. I was just pleased me, and Ben had helped save the world, but only we were going to know that.

An hour later, after driving along the freeway a while, I turned the radio on for some music.

"ABC and top of the news this hour ...
"Three teenagers, Benjamin, Jed, and Drew, are being interviewed by FBI agents in Jacksonville. The boys claim they have been abducted ..."

FORGIVEN

Hank Driscol was driving drunk when he was hit by another car. Nine years later, out of jail after being falsely charged by a crooked sheriff for something he is innocent of, Hank needs to deal with his demons and put the record straight.

Clean and sober, a member of AA, will Hank remember step nine and make amends to all those whose lives he damaged? More importantly, would he forgive those who damaged him?

Well ... maybe.

The rain had stopped at dusk, washing the pavement, leaving patches of rainbow water where oil caked the pavement by traffic lights. Wrappers, plastic cups, and empty garish card boxes whose contents were 'Finger Lickin Good,' overflowed from the sidewalk trash cans along Main Avenue. Nestling comfortably among the Pines, the town was just as I remembered.

A shopping mall surrounded by restaurants, bars, and banks dominated the center. Suburbia spread out either side along the freeway.

I had left the ferry at Bremerton and was looking for a motel and restaurant on the outskirts. I could see to things the following morning. They could wait - my stomach couldn't. The bus pulled into a parking lot next to Danny's Diner and a grubby motel that advertised vacancies with a tired looking neon flasher sign. I tossed the bus ticket they had given me at the prison into a bin and walked into the packed diner.

"Hi, there. Table for one?"

I smiled back at the woman's frozen smile. "A table and a menu, please."

She found me a small booth in the far corner and handed me a menu. Moments later, a young waitress appeared with the same silly smile through red lipstick.

I flicked the dog-eared menu over quickly and noticed a face at the bar I knew well. I felt a surge of anger as old memories caught fire. Of all the stinking bums I used to hang out with or those I usually avoided, this was one I wanted to meet...but not at that moment. Ignoring the man, I ordered.

"I'll take the mixed grill with over-easy eggs and can I get a bowl of fried onion rings ... nice and hot, please?"

The kid nodded, pouring me a coffee before she left.

She couldn't have been more than sixteen or so and the short skirt revealing too much thigh for her age made me uncomfortable. It was hard to picture Laurine after nine years, but I hoped she was a little more conservative.

Behind the waitress, the guy at the bar had seen me and was pushing his way toward me. I took a deep breath and thanked the girl.

"Well looky here at what the rain brought with it. I do hope you're passing through, you scumbag."

The same sarcastic sing-song tone from a voice I knew so well. The hair was well groomed, and the mustache trimmed above the thick pouting lips. The only difference was a bigger belly, and a Sheriff's shield replacing the old Deputy star. Sheriff Pecora, the face at the bar, removed his cap and squeezed into the booth. Wheezing, he pointed a stubby finger at me.

"No one wants you here after what you did. You put one foot over the line, and I'll run your ass outta town so fast your goddam feet won't touch the ground. You hear me?" His finger was tapping the table loudly and attracting an audience. "I'll be lookin' out for ya."

He slid out of the booth sideways and grunted as he stood. Glaring at me, he pushed his way back out of the bar.

Nine years seemed a lifetime, and no matter what, people only remembered the verdict and sentence. No-one cared about appeals. It took a long time for the nightmare of the tragedy to fade before I got a night's sleep.

"Ya mind if I join ya?"

An old man dressed in old denim overalls and a worn jacket didn't wait for an invite. His unshaven grizzly face and bright eyes and a mug of coffee in one hand told me we shared the same precarious slice of life. The one that taught those succumbing to temptation the art of redemption and survival.

With a toothy grin, he held out a weathered, leathery hand. "I'm John Brinton, and you're Hank Driscol. I'm on the ninth step of the program, and before the Lord, I'm here to make amends and tell you the truth."

The kid arrived with my dinner and a bowl of onion rings. Sliding the plate in front of me, she gave John a quizzical stare.

"It's okay," I said, forking the eggs. Yolk ran over some crispy bacon while John helped himself to an onion ring and winced as he burnt his fingers. More interested in eating, I spread the yolk before quickly stabbing my fork in his direction. Without looking up, I said, "He's with me although he won't be if he does that again. Why don't you freshen us up."

She disappeared into the crowd at the bar to retrieve the coffee pot.

"Okay, John, so besides getting a free coffee and stealing my food, what the hell are you selling?"

John slurped his coffee while I ate. I didn't call him by

his surname as we both belonged to AA.

"Nine years ago, Hank, at the accident. I got to you first but couldn't help. I know what I saw, though. I should have stayed."

He held his mug out for the waitress, his brow wrinkled with worry by thoughts of that day.

Memories flooded through my head, but John's face wasn't among them. What I remember was Pecora, an empty bottle of JD in his hand and his face peering at me through the shattered window, growling, "You're gonna' pay for this. I'm gonna' see ya in hell."

"I should have stayed," John said again, "but my son dragged me away. You can't blame him."

I looked up as he reached across the table and grabbed my arm.

"So sorry, Hank. I know ya didn't do it."

That night that changed my life came crashing back at me. Some memories sharply focused, others hazy. I remembered some things but nothing about John. He was a complete stranger.

***

New Year's Eve was like any other eve except for the kind of people out drinking. By the time they started to sing and act stupid they became pretty generous. I'm not a mumper, but when the dough runs out, and you're in another world, you sit next to an idiot who wants to buy everyone a drink. That's what happened nine years ago.

"Hey man, you've got an empty glass."

My neighbor didn't wait for an answer. With a click of two fingers that did a pirouette in mid-air, turning into a downward stab at our glasses, he nodded at the bartender.

"Happy New Year," I slurred.

The guy was a city office type and loaded. Two glasses later, he left, and I decided to go home.

Then Pecora collared me. "Where're your keys, Hank?"

The Deputy issued four counts of drunk and disorderly and one DUI over three years since my wife and kid ran out. That wasn't an excuse for getting drunk; I was just less cautious and didn't give a damn after they left.

I looked blearily into Deputy Pecora's eyes. "I'm walking tonight," I lied. "It's not far."

Minutes later, I pulled out of a side alley and onto Main Street. There was a turning to the right, up ahead. As I passed it, my world exploded, and everything went black.

The foggy recollection cleared from my head as John recounted his version of events.

"I was drivin' down Main toward you with my son as you reached the turning. That car shot out and walloped you good, man."

John's gravelly voice rambled on while I finished my dinner. There wasn't much he could tell me that I didn't know already, apart from the fact he saw who hit who first. That should have been obvious to the police at the time anyway, seeing the extensive damage and the position of the cars, but Pecora had it in for me. I was the town drunk.

What I really needed was to find the other driver and get an admission of responsibility. Revenge wasn't my motivation. The sentence was served and sobriety was changing my outlook on life. I wanted my license back. I couldn't use cabs forever. Trouble was, I would need to tiptoe around Pecora.

We left the diner and I headed for the Motel. I got the impression throughout dinner that John had something to tell me, other than an admission that he ran away from the accident.

"It's funny how the memory plays tricks with you when you get sober," he mumbled, shaking my hand. "I thought this might help you." From his pocket, he pulled a creased piece of paper. "It's the number of a local paper. You need to find out how to get in touch with a retired columnist, Helen Brind. She knows about the driver, and what he was up to on the night he crashed into you." John paused and looked around. "Be careful. My number's on the bottom if you want me."

He held onto the note as I reached out.

"Avoid Pecora, he's a dangerous man and not what he seems. They made him Sheriff after you went away."

***

"Can you let me have the number for Helen Brind?"

"She retired a year ago. Lives in Seabeck, I believe, but I don't have any details."

"It's a small place. Surely you-"

There was a click, and that was that. I thumbed through some notes on Brind that were the result of an hour's work at the local cyber café. The woman was a political journalist, well known for digging out dirt on City Hall in Bremerton and becoming a blunt needle in local government's ass. I could love someone like that.

On a hunch, I called John.

"Hi, John. I need another number or an address. I know you're worried, but I won't tell if Pecora asks. I know you've got a secret you'd rather have someone else tell me, but Brind's old office is telling me zip."

There was a pause, then, "Take the first turning right past Babs diner and the jetty. Go to the dead end. Brind's in the white house to your left hidden under the trees."

"I need a lift, John."

"Give me a few minutes."

Thirty minutes later, we stopped short of the house. Pecora's Lincoln was leaving the drive.

"Good job we missed him," mused John.

"Well, well, looks like today is open house for all the scum and down an' outs around here."

Helen Brind didn't mince her words. I could understand why she had a reputation as a firebrand. A bony hand waved us into the house, and as the screen door squeaked and clattered shut behind us, she led us into her kitchen. Grey hair tied tightly back into a ponytail accentuated a long wrinkled sallow face that lit up as her green eyes opened wide. Her small stature, heavily lined face, and age that I guessed to be around sixty lied about her fitness. A pile of split firewood by the stove testified to that.

"I take it you told him to come see me because that other fat dickhead has been scarin' you?"

She pointed at me as she faced John.

"Actually, ma'am, I came to-"

"You shush ya mouth and sit, son," she drawled dismissively at me. "I know why you're here."

John shuffled from one foot to another as Helen finished scolding him for bringing me there.

We sat and waited while she rolled a cigarette, lit it and picked off a strand of tobacco from the tip of her tongue.

"Pecora gave you a warning just like the one he just gave me." She waved my silence as our eyes met. "I know you've got a lot of questions, but I want you to promise no violence after I give you some answers."

I nodded as she rucked the knees of her worn, holed jeans up a little before crossing her legs. "Do you remember the Bremerton marina fiasco?"

It was hard not to. It all kicked off about the time of my accident.

Smoke drifted from Helen's nostrils.

"Two public inquiries listened to residents' complaints; both disregarded as contractors' bids were accepted. Then, through my sources and column in the Silverdale Post, I highlighted fraud and corruption in City Hall that involved a City Hall lawyer privately investing in one of the bidding companies. He was fired. Another contractor won the bid."

She coughed and snapped her fingers in the air. "All done - or so we thought. Everything came undone for the real villain of the piece when I found out the lawyer fronted a secondary smoke screen to cover the real fraud. The company that won the bid is owned by the mayor through a holding company."

"So ... what has this got to do with me?" I asked.

"Everything," she answered. "My photographer covered the crash, and one picture revealed a City Hall folder lying on the floor of the other car. It was titled, Marina. The injured guy was pulled out as my man arrived."

"I just don't remember." I shook my head.

"Well, I do. By the time the mayor's henchman Pecora was finished the file was gone, and so was the driver."

"But the driver was injured, surely?"

"The guy taken out of the car was in the back seat."

"So the driver did a runner, but he must have known the cops would catch up with him, so why run?"

Helen Brind cackled while she drew on the rolled cigarette hanging from her lips.

"I'd run if I knew my daddy would keep things quiet,

even more so if I were up to no good on his behalf."

"Bloody hell," I muttered. "The mayor's son?"

"You got it. All Pecora had to do was pin a dangerous driving sticker on your ass. With your previous, the mayor was home and dry."

She blew smoke into the air, her eyes locked onto mine. "He ain't worried about you either. He's got insurance on your tongue."

"How?"

"Laurine."

My daughter's name hit me like a sledgehammer.

John looked away, his fingers fidgeting with the ballcap in his hands.

Laurine was why he wanted me to see Helen, too scared of Pecora to tell me himself.

Helen tapped the air with a long forefinger, stopping me from jumping up. "She's eighteen and old enough to sleep with whoever she wants. She started dating the mayor's son, Gary, a couple of years ago when the marina opened for business. Now the pair is inseparable and spend a lot of time on Moonbeam."

Angry and confused, I needed to see Laurine and put her straight. That bum dating her was eating a knuckle sandwich if I had anything to do with things.

"In case you're wondering, Laurine knows all about the fraud. In fact ... not that I can prove anything since I retired ... she and Gary are supposedly very busy working with a conservation group, funded by City Hall, reporting on Orca Pods in the Puget Sound and the effect increased shipping has on their habitat. I think that's a bullshit cover for a very lucrative operation run by the mayor."

"Please don't tell me my daughter's mixed up with …"

Helen nodded. "My source works in the marina. He's never wrong. Trouble is there are too many palms being greased for the DA's office to do anything. They need hard proof, information on a pick up from whatever ship or yacht is bringing the stuff in so they can organize a raid. Your problem is Laurine. The first sign of trouble and the big boys will point at her, helped by Pecora. That's life for her, and you know what that's like."

"Yeah! He knows what that's like and he's going back the first chance I get."

We all jumped as Pecora crashed through the door.

"You thought I didn't know you were skulking around."

I felt the first blow as his fist crashed into the side of my face. The second landed on my nose as he stood in front of me. The third I didn't feel. I blacked out. I came around minutes later.

"Christ, you look a mess, son," mumbled Helen.

"I'll get those S.O.B's."

Helen smiled. "It's the only way to get your license back."

***

A pigeon waddled past the open door and stopped, its head jerking back and forth at me as though it was suffering from St Vitus dance. I threw a potato chip at it. There was a fluttering of wings as half a dozen other pigeons scrambled to fight for the morsel.

A pitter-pattering of raindrops hitting discarded burger cartons on the edge of the tarmac parking lot heralded another shower. After tossing the empty container into an overflowing bin, I closed the door and sat back, sucking diet Pepsi out of a giant cup.

John had been quiet ever since we left Helen's place. I could tell he was pretty cut up about Pecora but the look in his eye as he spoke said volumes to me. It had taken a moment's violence to convince him to overcome his fear.

"We need to deal with that swine. There's many a man, and woman too, who'd turn away if they saw anythin' they shouldn't," he'd said as we pulled into the burger stop.

"That's not the answer," I'd replied. "What I have to do is find the guy who was injured so we can bring the mayor's house down. If we do that I get to help Laurine out of trouble, clear my name ... and get my frickin' license back."

A short while later, John picked and sucked burger from his teeth as mist-like rain blew through the open window. I wound mine up.

"What we gonna' do now, then?" he asked.

"Go to the local newspaper. They should have the name and telephone number of the man I want."

It didn't take long to check the old newspaper reports on the court case. The man I wanted to talk to was one hundred thousand better off from insurance, and after further enquiries, I found he was living on disability payments. The man was living well.

An hour later, John pulled up outside the downtown address.

"You stay here and sound the horn if Pecora or his boys appear," I said, jumping from the car.

I left John keeping an eye out and quickly walked up the path to Dave Kingsman's small house. The girl at Silverdale Post had been hesitant but gave in when I explained who I was and that I sought Mr. Kingsman to make amends as in step nine of my AA program.

"Yeah ... who is it?"

A large tabby cat poked its head through a hole in the bottom of the net screen in front of the open front door. A man's voice came from the other end of the hall.

"Mr. Kingsman?" I enquired.

A small guy appeared and approached, a dishcloth he'd been using still in one hand.

"That's me. What d'ya want?"

You know, sometimes the smell of rats hits you without warning and Kingsman smelt really bad.

I pushed the screen and stepped inside. "I'm Hank Driscol, and my conscience brought me here straight from prison. I feel glad to see you. How do you feel?"

The color in Kingsman's face drained. "I guess I knew this day was comin' and you'd be after me."

"All I want is an explanation and for you to put the record straight with the Feds. Don't worry about Pecora or the mayor."

Visibly shaking, he motioned me in. "They said they'd kill me if I squealed."

"I was the chauffeur for Mayor Schmidt. After working for him for several years, he knew I knew things about him and his son ... things he didn't want anyone else to know about. He got me hooked the same way he got the rest of his puppets - by bribery, blackmail, and corruption. I passed a few dud cheques while going through a divorce, and he made it all go away."

Kingsman cuffed sweat from his brow. "That's how he got me." He slumped back into an old armchair. His cheeks glowed red as though he had run a mile, but nervous tension and beads of sweat on his forehead accompanied by small piercing dark eyes that darted back and forth showed the real reason. He was scared as hell.

"So, Dave, what happened on the night?" I asked.

His hands were shaking as he unscrewed a bottle top and raised the plastic container to his lips.

"Schmidt wanted to know about the bidding from two other competitors on the marina. Even as mayor, he was not allowed access to that information. Gary, his son, was told to break into the City Engineers Department and find the bid information so Schmidt could outbid them by noon the following day. That was the deadline. The trouble was I was pissed that night, so Gary drove. He wanted me to look out from the car park and warn him by cell if anyone turned up including the cops. If they did, I had to call Pecora to handle things."

Dave's hand shook and constantly fidgeted between resting on his lap and the arm of the chair. His voice wavered.

"We got away with the info, but Gary had his foot down. He was nervous and not paying attention. The rest you know, except what Pecora did."

"What?" I asked.

"Gary ran away and told me to stay put and call Pecora. I could hardly move anyway as one leg was jammed behind the front seat. When Pecora arrived, he had a bottle of JD in his hand. It was not in your car. He brought it with him. His report to the DA said I was unlikely to walk again and he had a doctor write a medical report as well. That's how you were charged with DUI and second-degree murder."

"And so for all the years I've been away, Schmidt has run a profitable drugs business and hooked my daughter as insurance against me mouthing off."

"Fraid so, Hank."

"Do you know when another shipment is due?"

"Yeah." Dave cuffed sweat from his upper lip. "Tomorrow night. Schmidt's yacht is due at the marina around one a.m. But you'd better be careful if you plan on bein' there."

"Why's that?"

"His men have guns. Your daughter is always with them."

I thought for a moment. "I'm trusting you don't talk to Schmidt. I'll put a word in for you."

Kingsman paused. "I have to be there too."

I smiled grimly. "Then keep your head down."

***

"I don't know if this is an unexpected pleasure or you're gonna' be a pain in the butt."

Special Agent Cecil Hunter held out a hand as I was shown into his office. I had taken the ferry across the Sound to Seattle and walked the hill up to the FBI building on 3rd Avenue. Cecil and I were acquaintances more than friends. We met in the Washington State Penitentiary where he held an AA meeting twice a week and where he made me see a lot of sense after becoming my sponsor.

"Hi, Cecil. I've come to tell you a story," I said, dropping into an armchair. "When I'm finished I want to ask for your help with sorting out a 'go easy' ticket for my daughter, Laurine. A word with the DA perhaps, as she's maybe gonna' finger some big guns for you."

Cecil held up a hand as he sat. "I have no idea what you're talking about so why not start at the beginning?"

And that's what happened. I gave him the whole story and named names who could authenticate the facts.

"Everyone's willing to testify provided you can convince the DA to go easy on the Indians. It's the three big guns at the top and the suppliers you want. So whaddya say?"

Cecil peered at me over the rims of his glasses as he picked up a phone. "You go anywhere near that marina tonight, and I'll have you back inside. You leave this to me. I know Laurine will be in danger, but that's my responsibility, not yours."

He looked up as someone answered his call. "Yes, get me the Operations Chief. No now, it's urgent!"

***

"What's happening?' John shivered in the cold night air and shrugged the elements off.

We had arrived a few hours before the Moonbeam was due, according to Dave Kingsman's information, and found a spot on the ferry passenger walkway that overlooked the marina. I was concerned about Laurine and her safety. The Feds had interviewed Kingsman and let him remain part of the setup. Helen Brind had filled the agents in with all the dirt she had uncovered. She called me with the news and celebrated with a little cackle. I guess she was wrapping up her unfinished business regarding city hall and enjoying the thought of a byline that would end her career on a high note, albeit a few years late.

"Be careful of that bastard, Pecora, Hank. That slimy

swine ain't gonna' be finished until the cell door clangs shut. You be careful, boy, you hear?" she had warned.

***

We never saw any agents holed up anywhere, but I guess we wouldn't. Out in the Sound, the Coasties would have to be part of the operation too, but all was quiet.

Then, suddenly, I got the shivers too.

"Well, hello boys. I've been waitin' for you."

John and I froze. Dressed in civvies, Pecora had sidled up amongst a group of passengers.

"Walk."

The snub nose of a pistol poked into my back.

Accompanied by two other thug cops, Ben Pecora walked behind us to the passenger terminal and into the coach and bus area where two patrol cars were parked.

"You're going for a frickin' ride, boys, care of Bremerton PD. Get in."

The door of a third unmarked vehicle, a black Lincoln, swung open and the short dumpy figure of Mayor Schmidt emerged. Stepping onto the sidewalk, he buttoned his jacket, smoothed hair across a balding head, and turned to Pecora.

"You put this situation to bed and right now. I don't wanna see either of these two again nor that frickin' dame out in Seabeck. Go and bury that bitch and silence her gab."

Schmidt turned to me. "I do hope you've not done any-thin' stupid, like talkin' to the Feds. If you have and my plans are ruined, your silly daughter is gonna get one through the head."

He gripped my throat with one hand and snarled. "She's nothin', but a plaything for Gary and I might just fool around with her a little too before I have her dealt with. You understand, you schmuck?"

His nose was almost touching mine. I could smell whisky on his breath. Two beady dark eyes stared into mine. He was definitely not a man whose warning could be disregarded. I said nothing but looked him straight in the eye.

Yeah. I understood. His grip on my throat eased. As he walked away, I hoped he would evade capture by the Feds. Whatever happened, I was gonna' get even.

As Schmidt climbed back into his Limo, I followed John into the back of a patrol car. Pecora spoke to the driver.

"Take them to Seabeck and make sure they're secure. We'll deal with them tomorrow. They can all take the trip to Bainbridge ... not that they're going to reach the island." He scoffed and waddled slowly back to his patrol car, his heavy frame swaying from side to side.

John and I looked at each other without saying a word. The cops up front said nothing either. We took off and headed for Seabeck.

Helen Brind wasn't at home. I guessed she was in protective custody, but Schmidt wouldn't have known.

The cops were annoyed. Pecora told them to wait. As we were hustled into the house, John surprised them and shocked me. For an old timer, he moved pretty quick. In front of me, he stooped swiftly and pulled a pistol from an ankle holster and turned on the two cops.

"Okay, dickheads, you gonna throw your guns across the floor and cuff yourselves to that fire stove. Don't think of anythin' funny. The mood I'm in, I'll do the same to you as I do to a raccoon's ass. Move it!"

Two minutes later and we were out of there, driving Helen's Jeep.

"Make for the marina," I shouted, "while I call Agent Hunter and warn him."

John spun the wheel as we joined the main road. We accelerated over the small creek bridge, all wheels leaving the tarmac as we hit the hump. Time was short. My Laurine needed me, and I needed her.

***

Timed to arrive at slack water, the Moonbeam slipped silently under a moonless sky through the calm waters of the harbor entrance. Her sails were furled and outboard engine cut.

As she reached the first pontoon, a figure stood up at the stern. The small engine gurgled into life. Another figure, crouching and hidden from the other crew member's view, emerged from the cabin and without warning, jumped into the blackness. A loud splash cut through the calm stillness and the night turned to day in an instant.

Powerful lights imprisoned the Moonbeam. Outside the harbor walls, a Coastguard cutter moved in to block any attempt to escape.

A warning from the Harbor Master's control center echoed across the water. "FBI ... Stand to at the pontoon and prepare to be boarded."

Within minutes, Gary Schmidt stood cuffed on the pontoon as agents unloaded two large suitcases. In the Command Center, Laurine sat covered in a blanket, shivering.

"Well done, Laurine. The mayor is about to get woken up from his last comfortable sleep for some time, and a few others are getting rounded up." Agent Hunter patted her shoulder.

"What about my dad? Seven years ago, you said you'd look after him if I worked for you. Where is he now?"

"I wish I knew," Hunter answered. "I have a feeling he's focused on hooking one big fat fish. I just hope he doesn't do anything stupid. I warned him to go home." He reached for his cell phone. "I'll try calling him."

Laurine looked anxious and whispered. "Please dad, be safe. I've missed you." A tear rolled down her cheek.

***

After warning Cecil Hunter that Pecora and Schmidt had

taken John and me prisoner and threatened Laurine, Cecil insisted he had everything under control.

I knew someone who wasn't, and that was Sheriff Pecora.

"I'm gonna' get that fat honker if it's the last thing I do." I looked sideways at John and shouted above the wind and whine of the engine. "The harbor's full of hidden blue bellies. Make for Bremerton police H.Q. According to Kingsman, Pecora receives the shipment there and drives it to a lockup."

A large black Lincoln passed as we drove around a bend. John banged the steering wheel. "That was Pecora. Those two thugs must have hidden a cellphone about them."

I looked back over my shoulder just in time to see the Lincoln swerving to a halt. He knew the jeep.

"Foot it. Let's get to the harbor. He doesn't know about the takedown tonight or that we've made statements to the Feds already. If he thinks that, then he's gonna' try and get rid of us."

As if to prove me right, a bullet smashed into the wing mirror my side, sending shards of glass and metal fragments into the air. The jeep veered across the road, narrowly missing an oncoming car.

John handed me his pistol.

"Much better to be in prison for parole violation than in a wooden box care of Pecora. That bum fires again, fire back."

Another bullet pinged off the back of the jeep. We both

ducked.

I turned and fired back at the Lincoln, a few feet from our rear fender, swerving back and forth across the road. Pecora lent sideways and held a pistol outside his window, pointing it at us. His face was lit from below by a green glow from the dashboard in front of him. I could clearly see the distorted look of hatred on his face. The jeep lurched down and up a pothole at the side of the road as I fired again. In that instant, I saw a flash and felt a sudden searing pain in my left arm. Some glass shattered by my seat.

John screamed above the cold wind. "You're hit! Shall I make for the hospital?"

"I'm okay! Just a crease!" I wasn't sure if it was or not, but I didn't want to stop.

John looked briefly down between our seats. "Damn bum got my JD as well!"

We were fast approaching Silverdale and Main Street. There were six sets of traffic lights and then a run to a sharp right-hander. Fortunately, at that time of night, there was very little traffic.

"Go for it," I shouted. "If we can run the lights he'll have to slow down at the right-hander. I can shoot one of his tires out."

John nodded and stabbed the pedal. A peel of thunder rent the air and seconds later, tires were hissing. We were drenched. Wipers flapped without effect.

Speeding behind us, Pecora turned the blues 'n' two's on,

the wailing siren pumping adrenalin and sharpening our senses.

"Two more to go," I shouted as we sped across an intersection.

Our Jeep slewed sideways, narrowly missing a truck crossing in front of us. Pecora slowed, putting more distance between us. Up ahead loomed the sharp turn to right although the rain was making it impossible to see clearly.

I tapped John's shoulder. "Take the corner fast and spin us around, so we face him. He'll have to slow."

Two wheels left the tarmac as we turned the corner. We slewed and juddered to a halt facing the oncoming limousine as it appeared - coming too fast. It careered across the road and stopped as it rolled onto its side.

"Stay here, John. I'll go see. Call agent Hunter."

I approached the limo. Pecora was scrambling through the smashed windshield.

"Well, this is your last night of freedom," I said, pointing the gun.

John joined us and took the gun. Pecora slumped, soaking wet to the ground.

"They ain't got nothin' on me, and neither have you. I'm gonna' get you, Driscol. You're frickin' dead," he growled.

"Oh yeah," said John. "You smashed my bottle, so I'll share it with you. He produced the bottle of JD from the Jeep and splashed it over Pecora.

I laughed. "The feds will get you alright, but I forgive you for drink-driving and for shooting at me, but I don't think the D.A. will ... not for ten years."

A siren wailed behind us, and soon we were joined by several patrol cars. Agent Hunter took one look at me and the gun I still had in my hand. I quickly handed it to John.

"Just holding it while he took care of a broken bottle," I said.

Hunter gave me a knowing look. "Good, because you need two hands right now." He stepped sideways as Laurine rushed forward and grabbed me.

"I got something for you, dad," she sobbed. In her hand, she held a driving license. It had my face on it.

THE LEPER'S SECRET

Nearly half our lives are filled with sadness and some-times fear. Families and friends are torn apart by lack of understanding or false belief through ignorance. By the time truth prevails, it is too late most times for a happy ending, as in this instance.

It was a lonely place that exuded a feeling of sadness and decay; of past pain and isolation. A thunderous sea and wind completed the scene, adding an undulating back-drop of power. It left me with a feeling of frailty ...

I cannot remember the exact awful detail of my father's execution, but my mind's eye revisited the gallows at Castle Green in Oxfordshire in many nightmares. In an early morning cold mist, I remember him being dragged through the castle gates and onto the green where he mounted the steps to the gallows with unsteady feet.

My grandfather's hand stopped me from seeing more.

The tall gray weathered castle walls echoed with the wails and shouts of the baying crowd as my father's life ended with a dull audible thud.

My grandfather led me away, clutching my hand as we pushed through the rowdy crowd.

At nine years of age, my only feelings were that I had lost both my parents, one murdered by the other.

The old man gave no thoughts on the matter, no explanation, save a warning that I grow to be a God-fearing man and not a sinner like my father.

It was an extraordinary experience for a young boy; such was my grandparent's anger and vilification of my father that I never cried over his death then or ever since.

The circumstances of my mother's death were shrouded in much mystery to my young mind. I remembered the last time I saw her she was unwell with a cold.

At that time in my life, I saw little of my parents as they worked all hours. My grandmother would visit each day at dawn, and look after and school me. Then, one day, as I recall, mother vanished.

My father told me she had gone away. It was shortly after this that the jailers arrived with a magistrate and arrested him. He was accused of murder.

In overheard conversation, I learned that despite my mother's body never being found, the authorities' suspicions determined my father was responsible for her assumed death on the word of my grandfather. This subject was never discussed again in my presence.

For the most part, I spent my young life confused and ignorant of the events that led me to live with my grandparents until I was eleven years old.

My grandparents were strict but generous, and after moving me into their home for two years, they sent me to a boarding school that I might 'fill my mind with useful knowledge.'

Several years later, both had passed away and left me a handsome amount of money. This generosity allowed me to concentrate on running a profitable business before any thoughts of a wife and family. My English teacher, a Mr. Marchill-Merriman, staunchly advocated that a young gentleman should strive to gain a professional position in life with adequate compensation before contemplating a family life. I must confess that whilst agreeing with his point of view, I enjoyed a bachelor's life, and the thought of marriage rarely entered my mind.

My good fortune allowed me to dress like a gentleman, a far cry from that time in my life when my shoes leaked and paper lined the soles. My hair, now cut and curled in the same style as Prince Albert and my starched shirts and modern morning coat were a far cry from shoulder-length hair and ragged clothes of my infancy. Despite this agreeable lifestyle, my parents were never far away from my thoughts, and I strived to immerse myself in friendships that kept them at bay.

***

And so it was with some concern one winter's day that I noticed my friend, Doctor Elliot Hume-Frobisher, casting caution to the wind, and indeed the rain, as he rushed across the muddy Kensington High Street. Hanson cabs drawn by blinkered skittish horses narrowly missed one another in the street. It was, indeed a most dangerous place to cross where the unwary could slip on mounds of slippery horse droppings.

   With one hand holding the edge of his top hat and the other waving his cane up at my office window, he stumbled up onto the footpath out of harm's way. His hasty actions brought several vulgar shouts from the cabbies, but he dismissed them and plunged headlong through my street door which was inscribed with gold lettering –

Wilber Wainwright
Accountant - Bookkeeper

I strode across the office and past Mrs. Gribben, my clerk, to the door. On opening it, I stood at the top of the stairs as Elliot slammed the street door below. Removing his hat, and depositing his cane in the rack stand, he doubled over wheezing heavily.

"Wilber ... I cannot believe it ... a strange occurrence, sir ... strange indeed. I have left my nurse in charge. That's how important it is, Wilber. I came as soon as I could."

"Calm yourself, Elliot," I chided. "You would do yourself much harm if such a state were not rested. Please take care and let us have tea while you recuperate."

Doctor Hume-Frobisher was a small but portly man of thirty-four years, while I was some ten years younger and taller. Unfortunately, due to a generous income that rewarded his skills in medicine, he had tended to over-indulge in wine and plentiful food that contributed to an unhealthy body his patients would have been ashamed of.

His red cheeks puffed out as he mounted the stairs. He rested at the top and flattened and combed his long silver hair with both hands. Drops of rainwater fell onto the shoulders of his black morning coat.

"Wilber, I need you to recount the circumstances of your mother's disappearance. I am here to convey to you news of her whereabouts."

After helping Elliot to a chair, I am sure that of the two of us I felt more shocked at his outburst than he was excited at his discovery. It had been a long time since I had sought any thoughts of my mother.

I rarely thought of my mother, not because I was devoid of any love for her. It was more because of her sudden disappearance followed by the imprisonment of my father and was the reason for my traumatized state at the time.

It had taken many months to overcome my deep depression, and I much preferred to dismiss any dark memories of that period to the back of my mind. Yet, despite this, and a good circle of friends, I could not rid myself of the nightmare of Castle Green, but lived in hope it would slowly fade as I grew older.

As Mrs. Gribben poured our tea, I sat with impatience, my right heel tapping the floor. Elliot mopped his brow and waved his lace kerchief in the air. We were immediately engulfed in the scent of lavender.

"Come now, Elliot," I encouraged as he accepted a cup, "Take a sip and relax. Expand on your revelation, so I am able to understand how your information furthers my life story."

Elliot sipped at the rim of the cup, his thick red lips making a loud sucking noise. "Well," he said at length, "Did your mother have much to do with your daily upbringing?"

I shook my head at this unexpected question. My mother worked with my father on most days, making tables and chairs, mostly for the working class. It was my grandmother who dressed and washed me and schooled me and offered comfort when I fell over or became ill. My grandfather, a very stern and religious man, stayed out of my grandmother's way most times. He recognized that it was the woman of the house who looked after things domestic and his place was to admonish those who did not meet his cleanliness and Godliness expectations.

"That answers a perplexing puzzle, dear Wilber." Elliot averted his eyes to the window, looking, I thought, a little shame-faced. "Before she disappeared, was your mother in good health or did she have any red sores or lesions upon her skin?"

"What on earth?" I replied indignantly. "No – she had no marks and was in good health although I do remember she had been suffering from a cold that returned several times that year. Why are you making such strange inquiries?" The embarrassment I felt was quite acute, especially as we were talking in front of Mrs. Gribben.

Elliot picked up and examined my fountain pen, a new writing aid that was fast replacing the dip pen. "My first patient this morning has come from Yorkshire and is in London on business. He is the honorable Mr. Felton Kirkman esquire, head administrator of Harper Fields Hospital that stands outside the coastal town of Whitby."

"So what is he to do with my mother?" I asked.

"He saw the photo I have on my mantle of you and your mother, and he recognized her. I recounted your tragic story, and he told me something that shook me to the core, sir."

The suspense was such that I held my breath for by this moment I expected the worst possible news.

"A gravedigger that was in his employ recently moved down to his birthplace at Dunwich on the Suffolk coast."

Both Mrs. Gribben and I paused, not unlike statues. Such was our expectation of a great surprise.

"He buried your poor mother, not more than a year ago."

I gasped and raised one hand to cover my mouth while Mrs. Gribben, for fear of fainting, grasped my other hand with hers whilst her eyes looked upward and closed.

"Dear God," I cried at last. "I cannot believe this. I do not understand. What happened that I suffered being abandoned by a mother who willingly let my father go to his death on the gallows?"

This revelation brought sharp images of that fateful day at Castle Green, and I shuddered.

Elliot patted my shoulder. "You are as shocked as I and your course is clear. Inquiries must be made of this man. This will be deeply depressing for you, but one cannot disregard the information without getting to the truth of the matter."

His fingers lightly gripped my shoulder.

We both stood in silence for a moment. Mrs. Gribbens sat with head in hands, now and again uttering, "Oh my, oh my."

I agreed I would make arrangements to make a hasty journey to Dunwich.

"It will be a long sober journey across the countryside too Ipswich and then on to Dunwich so take warm clothing and an umbrella," Elliot advised. "The weather in Eastern Anglia is most inclement at this time of year."

***

Two days later, with much on my mind, I took the carriage from London to Ipswich and found Elliot's advice correct. Sheets of rain slammed into us. As it hit the sills of the open windows, spray spat at me, stinging my face. It was indeed, a long and uncomfortable journey. I changed coaches in Ipswich and arrived on the Suffolk coast at dusk, spending the night at the coaching inn.

I found Dunwich to be a desolate place of sparse populace. On a bright day, the village probably had the charm to encourage visitors to walk and take the sea air as our Queen had invited her subjects, telling us the air greatly aided those with Tuberculosis and a host of other ailments. On this day the sky was cluttered with overlapping black clouds that moved slowly, blown by a stiff wind.

After settling into lodgings, I took directions to St James's Church and the old leper chapel. Mr. Felton Kirkman had been quite concise in the carefully written instructions that he gave my friend Elliot.

The gravedigger, one Joshua Snipes, lived in one of the three small cottages that had survived decay since the church handed the care of leprosy over to the authorities in the late 17th century. The landlord assured me the best route was the coastal path for it afforded one the best view of what was left of St James's.

The coast walk was cold and uninviting. Huge white-crested grey waves crashed with a thunderous roar up onto the gravel beach below before leaving sheets of foam as they retreated. This did nothing to encourage my enthusiasm. I pulled a thick cloak across my chest as the biting wind blew strands of hair across my eyes and numbed my ears and the tip of my nose. I screwed my eyes but that did little to stop the wind from making them water. Below me, along the shore, brick debris showed above the waves as the water receded each time.

For many years, the sea had gradually swallowed up half the village as the cliffs eroded, leaving scattered remnants of the past to rot and disappear in the sand and shingle.

As the church came into view, my mood darkened. There were many questions to be asked, and the thought that some dark secret had been kept from me made me determined to seek out Snipes to ease my concerns and learn the truth about my parents.

The west wall and the chapel stood next to the foundations of the colony - all overgrown with weed; the stone ruins partially covered in green algae. Grey stone and white marble lay in piles where it had fallen. Thick with red rust, door handles, locks, hinges, and iron bars from the windows were half- buried all about and from every crack sprouted tangled tall grass and weeds that lay bent forever by the fierce winds.

It was a lonely place that exuded a feeling of sadness and

decay; of past pain and isolation. I stood thinking of my mother and father. Despite the whistling wind and thunderous sea that completed the scene, I could still hear the ghostly shouts and screams of Castle Green that would not leave my head. The dark and powerful landscape left me with a mixed feeling of awe and frailty.

**

Three little whitewashed cottages stood in a forlorn huddle not far from the other side of the church. Smoke blew swiftly sideways and down into the yard from one of the stacks. I hurried down a sloping path from the clifftop and walked to the cottage door. Much of the paint had peeled away, and the wood beneath had long started to weather and rot. I wrapped my knuckles on the door and almost at once the door latch clicked.

"You be welcome, Sir, although I suppose you to be more of a gentlemanly nature by the look of your dress and used to finer living. My home be small and oft times cold, but you are bid welcome to tea and crabcake. Come sit you by the fire."

Mr. Joshua Snipes was an old man of sixty or more, and despite his apparent poor status and ragged clothes, I warmed to his cheery disposition. Of thin build, his body had not bent with age, and his arms and kneck showed much strength.

Rubbing my hands before the fire, I waited for him to sit. "I come on an errand of much importance, Mr. Snipes, and hope you will have much information for me."

With the certainty that I could trust him, I recounted my story, making sure of every detail while he nodded knowingly.

Sucking on his clay pipe and pouring tin mugs with tea, Snipes began a narrative that was to change my life from that moment on.

Joshua Snipes, or Josh as he privileged me like his friends to call him, was an unusual man in many ways. As we settled down in front of his wood fire, the glow from the grate highlighted his weather-beaten face and red cheeks. Age had marked him but not with sallow cheeks or sullen looks like the poor. His was a face at peace which displayed a somewhat wise and educated look.

Our shadows stretched across the small parlor and climbed the grubby white lath and plaster wall behind us. A shock of long silver hair fell over Joshua's shoulders. Smoke from his pipe drifted above his head, and through the grey smokey whisps, two bright twinkling blue eyes peered at me intently, as though he were looking into my very soul.

"You be asking about your Mater, and I note you nay mention your Pater. Why is that?"

He leaned forward as I straightened at the mere mention of my father. His large rough, calloused hand rested on my knee, the mass of wiry silver hair on its back raised in profusion.

"Josh, you must know that my father was hanged for my mother's killing, but if that is not the truth, I fear the guilt I am feeling for growing up thinking him to be evil. I have never been told otherwise."

Josh patted my knee. "Guilt is an emotion that will linger unless you conquer it. I know thee to be an honest and God fearing man so thank the Lord for the good news that your Pater was innocent and died for a good reason and that your Mater lived."

"I don't understand ..."

The old man held up a hand. I had not noticed until then that he wore a short beard that covered and curled under his chin. The hair below his lower lip was tinged yellow with the years of pipe smoking.

"I knew your Mater well enough from the day she arrived at our church and a more civil and caring woman I have never met. A beautiful woman she was but not so much in appearance but rather a deep beauty that filled her heart."

Confused and afraid that I might hear something that was unthinkable, I held my silence with bated breath.

"Of course, I knew nothing of her talk with Father Droon until much later, but from the first, we knew not to waggle tongues but keep our own company. Your Mater I met the day after her arrival; she was immediately taken into the hearts of all. She nursed those who needed the most care and worked day and night with us in the hospital. An angel that walked among the afflicted, if ever there was one."

I scarce believed what I was hearing.

"A nurse ... my mother a nurse? But what of my father? None of what you say is making sense to me. Did Father Droon know my father was to try for her murder?"

"Nay, young sir. Our Order knew nothing at first - not until much later."

"Your Order?" My first impressions of Josh were correct. He did not fit the glove of a gravedigger."

"I was a priest until I loved your Mater."

In the silence, the crackling wood in the grate and tiny red sparks of ash shooting upwards gave rise to an eerie feeling of mixed emotions. I sat forward but said nothing while rubbing my hands and feeling the heat on my face. Without looking up at Joshua, I knew he studied me while sucking his pipe.

"You be angry with me, and that be normal, but I beg you not judge me until you know all," he said at length.

"I do not judge you, Josh, but am indeed angry, more for my own acceptance that my mother was dead. I should have searched her out."

A long shrill whistle came from the cracked doorframe as fisting winds blew more intensely inland from the sea. A muffled bell rang in the distance. Josh crossed himself.

"A raging sea be brewing. The old Saint James bell and tower fell to sands a great many years ago, and now it be swallowed by water. Strong tides ring the bell for all the poor buried souls who were taken with it."

I crossed myself also, shivering at the thought of bones scattered on the seabed.

Josh tossed a rough woolen blanket into my arms.

"You be needing that if you are to hear the truth of your Mater, for it will take the night to set your mind at ease although I doubt you will be satisfied."

Handing me a small earthen pot and wooden spoon, he poured steaming vegetable soup from a kettle settled at the side of the open grate.

I thanked him, took a lump of bread offered, and dipped the soup. "Please tell me, Josh ... tell me all."

Huddled close to the fire, we gazed into the flames as he spoke.

"Well now, it was late afternoon when a carriage arrived outside the church, and a woman of good build alighted."

Josh gave me a sideways glance.

"Not what one would call a lady of substance by her dress, but by the way she stepped across the track holding her skirts, a lady just the same. No carriage ever went into the courtyard, and so she walked to the rectory of Father Droon and entered as though expected. It was the following morning that Lianda visited our hospital and met myself and father Michael, my assistant."

Josh stopped for a moment to sip soup from his spoon.

"I take the liberty to call your Mater by her name and

shall do so from here on. It was at her request that I call her Lianda, something that fills my empty life with joy each time I think of her."

He breathed deeply.

"Plain but with a smile that lit the room, she spent time with each of those afflicted with leprosy. She also helped me in all duties as she became more experienced during that first year. My vows were strong, but love proved stronger, and despite her iron will, I knew she harbored the same feelings for me."

"Did you tell her?" I asked.

"Nay, not until after she was attacked and I took the life of Father Michael."

I am not sure I heard a faint sob above the spitting wood but looking into his glistening eyes, Josh could not mask his true feelings nor could he bear to return my gaze.

A great silence fell between us that begged he continued his story when his composure permitted. That it would take all night to recount the truth behind my mother's death, I had no doubt for he had so far barely told much. Josh seemed reluctant but determined to rid himself of something that weighed heavily upon his shoulders, and not without good reason. With soup finished, I prompted him with an inquiry that could wait no longer.

"Was my mother suffering leprosy?"

Josh sighed heavily. "Eventually, yes. At first, Lianda was fearful but not sure. It can be many years before the

disease shows itself and then after a year or two of incuba-
tion. Your Pater gave cause for her concern, and after you
were born, they were in agreement as to your upbringing.
A wet nurse weaned you, and your grandparents looked
after you much of the time while Lianda and your Pater
worked long hours to pay a nanny. As much as it caused
great pain, you were never kissed, nor slept with them."

It was true that my childhood was devoid of much attention from my parents and I often wondered as I grew older
if indeed they had regretted having a child.

"You say my Pater gave my Mater much concern. How
so? Do I guess correctly that he passed leprosy to her?"

"I think it better I continue from the beginning as I knew
nothing of Lianda's background until after that terrible
day of violence years later. It was that nightmare which
urged her to relate her tragic life to me."

My conscience pricked, I felt sadness and anger at never
having given my mother any thought as I grew up. I nodded at his suggestion and gazed back into the fire.

"We spent many hours caring for the sick and burying
them too. Lianda was a comfort to all including myself and
assistant, Father Michael. It was a year after she arrived
that we knew, without declaring for fear of breaking my
promise to God, that we were in love. Father Michael, it
was, who uncovered our feelings by watching us closely.
He threatened by words beneath his breath that if guilt
came the better of him, he would talk to the Abbot and

have Lianda sent away."

Josh closed his eyes. "I pray for forgiveness every night for keeping my brother's words silent. I feared Lianda would forsake me if she knew. It was a few months later that I heard her cries one night. On rushing to her room, I found Father Michael with her, his hands about her."

Lips tightly drawn, Josh's broad shoulders sagged, and his voice lowered to a whisper.

"Merciful God, I grasped a grate poker and crushed his head."

My breathing came heavy as Josh's revelation shook me. He had saved my mother but killed another unnecessarily. Instead of grappling with Father Michael, his fit of anger, tinged with possessiveness and perhaps jealousy, had made him forget his vows for one terrible moment.

"Then what happened," I enquired. "Surely there was a trial?"

"Nay. Father Droon it was who Lianda and I spoke to alone. Fearful that the church would transport him, along with myself, to a mission in the penal colonies, his actions were immediate. Lianda was sent to the chapel to pray for forgiveness while I took Father Michael to the lepers graveyard and buried him without a marker. In the morning, it was decided that Lianda was to stay and I was to give up my Holy Order and remain as a gravedigger. We were forbidden to meet or speak to each other again."

As he spoke with trembling voice, I saw a man much

troubled by an inner turmoil that haunted him. The release of a confession from his heart was so deeply felt that tears freely flowed from closed eyes.

"I saved the woman I loved and lost her at the same time," he sobbed.

There was still more story to come as I tossed logs onto the fire. With my inquisitiveness peaked and, as much as I appreciated Josh's state of mind, I was anxious to learn more.

"You say it was after this that she told you how she came to be at the hospital. There were moments when you did see each other, then?"

Josh produced a large handkerchief from his grubby waistcoat pocket and blew his nose with great ceremony. "Yes, we met once each month while Father Droon went to meet with the church heads in Colchester, yet it was still another two years before she spoke of you."

Outside the cottage, the crashing waves and howling wind were louder and the sad clanging of the entombed tower bell more frequent. The bedlam was unnerving. Somehow I felt that our surroundings were in keeping with the atmosphere Josh created with his narrative. My body shivered despite the warmth of the fire and blanket.

"Did she speak of me?" I asked.

"She did. She spoke of you as her 'untouchable child' though told me more of her husband as it was he who caused the misery she suffered. It was after this talk that

Mr. Kirkman arrived to replace the priests with nurses. The afflicted were encouraged to see visitors and write letters, something I welcomed. I could comfort Lianda more."

My heart sank. My earlier feelings were correct that I was indeed an unwanted child.

"Be not sad, Wilber, for your mother wrote about you to your grandparents when she was able."

Josh sighed deeply. "She also left a letter with Mr. Kirkman … for you."

"For me … but I do not have it."

"It's with Mr. Kirkman. You must see him in person now you have seen me."

Why Mr. Kirkman had not tried to find me and deliver my mother's letter was puzzling. In fact, when he consulted my friend, Elliot, and had seen a picture of my mother, he said nothing of such communication or Elliot would have informed me. It was also puzzling that my grandparents had hidden the secret from me after they knew my mother to be alive. Perhaps they were so ashamed.

"I think it best you rest until the day breaks, Wilber. There be no closed coach back this night, and the one to Ipswich leaves the village at eight or thereabouts. It might be prudent to carry a shilling too. Mr. Kirkman is, in my opinion, an honest and hardworking man but one who lives frugally and a shilling will be welcomed for his services."

I sat long into the night looking into the fire. There were decisions to be made about a murder and a wrongful hanging. Joshua Snipes sat alongside me and there being nothing else to say, we kept our thoughts to ourselves and spent a sleepless night wrapped in his ragged blanket.

In the morning we walked the cliff path to the village.

"You know where I be should you seek me, Wilber."

He stood, bent over with hunched shoulders, a sad and dejected looking figure, seeing my coach off without waving goodbye.

In Ipswich, I lodged for the night before boarding the first of two coaches taking me up north to the east coast town of Whitby.

The next two days were spent surviving the ordeal of a cold hostel bed and uncomfortable carriage travel through stormy weather. This experience filled me and cloaked my surroundings with a dark and gloomy atmosphere.

***

Harper Fields Hospital was uninviting and without any redeeming qualities. It lay back at the end of a gravel driveway, hidden behind the Norman church of St. Bartholomew. The building spawned ugliness, decay, and abandonment. There was something about it that filled one with a helpless feeling of futility, and yet the visible signs of cleanliness and order showed. Masses of chipped red brick, blackened with age, covered the walls but the ground around the building was clean. A grassed area smelling freshly cut to the rear of the church was fenced high, the only outdoors the patients were allowed to use.

"You are welcome here, Mr. Wainright, but for privacy and should your sensitive nature be offended at the sight of leprosy, I suggest we talk in the church."

Mr. Felton Kirkman was a robust, ruddy complexioned, kindly gentleman in middle age. Grey-green eyes peered at me through thick lens pince-nez glasses balanced near the end of his bulbous nose. His worn but smart plain black suit and frayed shirt collar confirmed Joshua's opinions.

With introductions over, he swept some stray hair back over his balding head with a quick hand motion and ushered me toward the church entrance.

"A note from Doctor Hume-Frobisher informed me that you were visiting Joshua Snipes and I assume Joshua told you of your mother and that his love for her betrayed his calling here."

He shook his head slowly as we sat. "A sad affair. That said, I have your mother's letter ... and a surprise I kept secret from your doctor. I had no idea how to find you until I went to see him."

I breathed deeply. "A surprise?"

"Yes, you have a sister."

The granite walls closed in as Mr. Kirkman faded from view.

***

"My dear Sir, are you well?"

The soft voice got louder as all around me gradually came into sharp focus. Never having fainted, the experience was quite confusing and frightening.

"I'm all right," I answered, looking down at my trembling hands, although I would have fallen if I had tried to stand.

"Perhaps we might wait until you are fully recovered before I continue to explain your mater's wishes."

Mr. Kirkman looked most concerned.

"No, please. I've been traveling and have spent an uneasy night in the company of a priest who has taken a life and related to me the upsetting story of my mother. Perhaps some food might do me well while we talk." I held out two shillings.

Mr. Kirkman smiled thankfully and with one hand under my right arm, helped me to stand.

"Then let us walk to my cottage at the other side of the grounds, and you shall eat rabbit and home-baked bread."

The cottage was small and sparsely furnished but clean and tidy. The white-washed walls reflected much sunlight shining through some latticed windows.

My stomach churned as the pleasing aroma of stewed rabbit wafted under my nose. In no time at all, we were sitting at the small dining table.

I tore a small wedge of crusty bread and dipped it into the stew as Mr. Kirkman spoke.

"Your mater made a strange request before she passed

away, in that I should tell, rather than request, that you open the letter she wrote you only after you met your sister. Of course, I do know where you will find Mary, for that's her name."

"And you have more to tell me about my mother?" I asked, chewing rabbit.

"Indeed. Your mater harbored a secret, only revealing it to Joshua and I on her deathbed."

From his pocket, Mr. Kirkman produced a long white envelope and placed it on the table, keeping his hand upon it.

"What I reveal now is her story, as told it to me. I cannot prove or disprove it for I was not there. However, I am sure of the facts, knowing her as I did as an honest and loving woman."

He sighed gently and withdrew his hand from the table.

"When your mater arrived, she was greeted by Father Droon. After relating her position to him, he took her in and within a short time she was nursing within the hospital. Joshua and Father Michael could not understand that your mater would give of herself freely. It was much later, after Father Michael's death, that the reason rested in an arrangement for care without payment. All next of kin had to pay whatever they could afford. Your mater had nothing."

"So she paid her care by nursing."

"No. When she arrived, she was accompanied under cloak by your sister, two years your senior. She is here."

Mr. Kirkman paused.

"I am sure your mater set everything out in the letter she entrusted to me. I know this revelation is yet another shock, but the truth reveals your mater as a truly remarkable and loving woman who went to extraordinary lengths to protect those close to her including your pater."

I shifted awkwardly and clenched a fist. "But my fathe-"

"Nay, Wilber ... say nothing of your pater, for if ever true repentance were shown by a sinner, it was paid in full by him."

"My mother's self-imposed sentence was far harsher than that of the man who forced her into it, surely?" I replied with impatience.

With a quiet and patient tone, Mr. Kirkman continued, his hands rested on the table as he slowly leaned toward me. "Your pater took up with a whore before your sister was born. The woman's passing of wetness of the lips and perspiring flesh caused him to carry the disease on to your mother and after she was born, Mary too. It was not until your sister was two years old that leprosy showed itself on her and your mother. By that time you were conceived and your parents, fearful for your safety, made plans for your upbringing through grandparents."

"So why did my father not accompany my mother and sister here?"

Mr. Kirkman shrugged. "I do not know, but I am sure the letter will explain. What I do know is that your mater said something strange and perplexing as she died - 'I love you, my dear husband, with my last breath and hope you forgive me.'

***

It was with an absolute dread that I stood before a large door marked with the word 'Visitor.'

"Mary cannot talk but does hear. She covers her head except for a fold where her eye can see you. I have told her you are here."

Mr. Kirkman opened the door and stepped inside, beckoning me. What was immediately apparent was a foul smell of disinfectant and as I turned into the bare white-washed room a single chair stood in the center and sitting upon it, a figure draped from head to toe with a large gray woolen blanket. Her body moved slowly back and forth accompanied by wheezing breath.

It seemed an eternity before I spoke. "Hello, Mary. I'm Wilber ... your younger brother."

The head turned, and I caught a glimpse of an eye as she nodded. "Perhaps I might hold your hand?" I asked.

Her head shook, and she turned away.

"Mr. Kirkman related how you and our mother came to be here. I am so sorry and wish I knew you sooner."

"She is without thought," whispered Mr. Kirkman. "She fights for air. Soon she will go."

Mary remained motionless. I left, feeling sad that I would never know her. I followed Mr. Kirkman into the grave-yard and under an overhanging tree was guided to a small wooden cross. Around the grave was freshly cut grass.

"This is your mother's grave," said Mr. Kirkman. "She is at peace, and your sister will lay beside her very soon."

I thanked him, and after spending a short time saying a prayer, I made my way back to my coach.

***

As my coach traveled to the railway, I opened the letter. The amazing testimony before me would change my life forever and make me a wiser man.

My dear son,

I ask your forgiveness and understanding in this, my confession. The Lord has seen fit to end my punishment and let me find peace in death.

The following letter is a true account, as best I remember it, of the sin that cast our family into hell and left you alone and without parental love.

Your grandparents who took great care of you were not privy to most of what you are about to learn here. Indeed, no-one except Mr. Kirkman knows of these contents.

Hitherto, they have been kept close to my heart.

Two years after Mary was born, after consulting our

doctor about some lesions on my skin, I knew about the Leprosy. He was sure I would not show outward signs for several years or more. Mary would also suffer due to our closeness and oft times sleeping in each other's arms. Being a month away from bearing you, I gave the grave news to your father.

Together, we decided that the social implications would commit myself and Mary to a terrible colony outside the city and for him, if devoid of the disease, a shunning from work and a life of misery in a poorhouse.

Our only concern was for Mary and yourself. For you, a life of ignorance until you commanded sense and under-standing and for your sister a place where she would be warmed by my love in peaceful surroundings. After you were born, your grandparents took you away, and for four years we met you on each Sabbath before you were sent to boarding school.

It was in your eighth year that my disease began to show. Through my doctor, I sought refuge at Harper Fields. Your father had agreed not to discuss my where-abouts, and so I started my life again, caring for the sick.

It was with great concern that I learned of your father's arrest, but he managed to send an instruction that for Mary and your sake, I remain silent.

Your grandparents were swayed by wagging tongues. They lay the blame of my disappearance at your father's feet for sinning with another woman while I was with *child and that, besotted with that woman, disposed of Mary and me.*

Your father went to his death a strong-willed man who showed much love and concern for his children. Within the spiritual silence of the hospital, I have kept the biggest secret of all that has been my punishment, for it was not your father who broke the seventh commandment - it was me. It was I who lay with another. My sin was the greater, for in your father's death, his silence saved Mary much misery and you the chance to build a gentleman's reputation.

Forgive me, Wilber, and remember your father as a good man. May your life be blessed with good fortune and health.

This was not the happy conclusion that I sought but a lesson in my mother's fortitude and love, and a lesson in my father's undying love for her, my sister and his son. Most of all, it was now my place to accept my responsibility to forgive those who kept me from the truth and become a gentleman my parents would be proud of.

Carefully placing the letter in my pocket, and with emotions overflowing, I held my head high and wept.

CUT

Have you ever wondered why many discerning murderers are never caught? It's because the people they despatch are never found. If you wanted to dispose of a body without detection, where would you go for help?

My breath turned to vapor as I waited. The night was bitterly cold, and the inside of the car had become a fridge. A film of ice was forming quickly on the inside of the windshield.

With a shrug of the shoulders, I turned the key, and the engine purred into life as always. It was the one thing that never let me down. The station wagon was the most important tool I had. Without it, there was no business.

I reached for the thermos flask as two bright headlamps turned into Forty-Third Avenue two blocks up. The boys were early, but it didn't matter too much. The gravel parking lot they were headed for was deserted and ideal for taking the delivery. I'd checked it out for the last few nights, and it had stayed empty.

Forty-Third was an empty area. It was lined by a few occupied workshops but mostly derelict warehouses that once served the disused docks they backed onto.

***

My career, if you can call it that, started when Tony Sparizza, a college buddy, bumped into me in my local supermarket during the summer recess of my final year. I say buddy, but that was only because he took my side when I got bullied. One of those sickly kids who never did P.E., I attracted bullies, and so I followed Tony and hung out with him and his gang.

It was in my second year that I found out that Tony's father was a 'made man.' My mom and dad didn't mind too much. They knew there was no way I would ever be a 'made man'. But I ended up being a gofer for the son of one. Several years later, Tony became 'made' himself.

My meeting with him in the supermarket that day was not by accident. He had been looking for me. He wanted to borrow my car, an old Chrysler I had saved for, over three years. I wanted to say no, but when Tony told me his father wanted it and would pay me fifty bucks, saying no was out of the question.

"It's okay, Joe," drawled Tony, guzzling a soda. "It's not for a job or anything like that. His car is in for service, and he wants to take mom to a party."

We drove back to my place, and I handed him the keys.

"You'll get it back clean," he said, before driving away.

The next morning I found the car in my driveway. It had been through a car wash. The inside was clean and smelled of seat polish and bleach. For a second, I thought the smell unusual, but that was just for a second. My mind was elsewhere when I found an envelope with fifty bucks inside on the front seat.

Over the next three years, I regularly loaned Tony my car. At first, he would tell me his car was getting serviced, or his dad had it. In the end, I wasn't bothered why he needed the car. At fifty bucks a time, who cared? It never occurred to me that I should be loaning the car for free to a friend. Tony was happy to pay.

As my twenty-first birthday was the same month as his, he decided we should celebrate together on his birthday. His father was paying, and it promised to be a great party. Plenty of 'made' guys were going to attend with their wives and girlfriends, plus all of Tony's street gang.

My mom and dad politely refused an invitation, saying that my dad would be on nights that week. He worked as a supervisor at the power station and couldn't stand the thought that his colleagues would find out about him drinking with the mob.

Compared to the upcoming party, my own family party was a real dull affair. Mom, dad, aunt Rene, and grandmother Brown sat around the dining room table reminiscing about my life so far and making a big thing about cutting an iced sponge cake decorated with the usual message and a large 21 across the middle. I wasn't surprised that Tony didn't arrive. I never expected him. He rarely came to the house and when he did it was to pick me up or drop off the car. Of course, I received handy gifts. My own decorated beer mug with my name on it from my parents together with a diary and a gold St Christopher bracelet. Yeah, bloody useless.

It was at Tony's that day of the party that I was given a chance to have a real job working for Tony's dad. After several years working in Jerry's D.I.Y. store for a pee-poor wage, I accepted right away.

"Happy birthday, Joe," said Tony, winking. "You'll get five hundred a month. You'll soon be looking like one of dad's crew."

At that point, I knew nothing about the job and was told to see Tony's dad the following day by 'Digger,' a giant of a man in his forties no-one liked to cross. Digger came from Brooklyn, with a voice like an old rusty file and a pair of hands as big as shovels. Rumor had it that he was a hitman, but of course, no-one knew for sure.

The following day, Tony picked me up. He was driving an old Cadillac and certainly looked the part with a pair of Rayburn's and cool casual outfit. I guess it was that day that I decided what to do with my life, but that decision was after I had seen Tony's dad who said everything, while at the same time, nothing at all.

"The first thing you gotta know, Joe, is that Tony had a special gift for his twenty-first. He's now a 'made' man.

The news took me by surprise, but later I realized it would be pretty obvious for Leon Sparizza to promote his own son.

Leon was a smart man, always in a suit although he never looked like a mob boss. A little over six foot tall, he was slim and had a shock of well-groomed silver hair. So after slapping Tony's back, I sat with him and listened while the boss told me about the job.

"Package runs for me, but in the main I want you to work with Tony doing what he wants."

"Thanks, Mr. Sparizza. What packages are being delivered?"

"Dead drops." He smiled. "No need for you to know more until later. Tony will fill you in as and when. Okay?"

"Yes, Sir."

And that was that. I was in with the boys. It took no time at all before Tony was showing me what the special 'Dead Drops' job was.

"Skimmers, snitchers, double-crossers, and disloyal members are always around, and the mobs are always having a clearout. The trouble is they have a problem getting rid of the dirt. Our boss provides a unique service. We take delivery, package the goods, and find a nice graveyard we can bury them in. There's a lot of dollars in this."

"You're joking," I said.

Tony became serious. "No. I know you well, and I told my dad we could pull this off. I've got a couple of other fellah's who are in, and all we have to do is find drop off points for delivery and dumping grounds for burial."

Back home as I lay, looking up at my bedroom ceiling, the enormity of what Tony and his dad were involved in got to me. I never worried about anything Tony wanted me to do. He always looked after me. Of course, now he was a 'made' man I knew he was into more serious stuff than selling knocked off phone cards, whiskey, and cigarettes.

Dead drops was another thing, though. Tony said there was no way we could get caught even if the cops found a body. Like ... the body couldn't be linked to us, especially if we wore gloves and kept our car clean. That was going to be my job - cleaning the car. The bodies, Tony said, came from all over. Even so, I laid awake all night and made up my mind to tell Tony I couldn't help him. I felt terrible at letting him down but shifting and burying bodies wasn't for me.

"Tony's outside for you," announced my mother as I walked into the kitchen. She pointed out of the kitchen window as a horn blared with impatience.

My stomach tightened. I took a deep breath. I hoped Tony

would understand and we would remain friends. Outside, as I walked toward Tony's car, I could see someone in the back. I froze. It was 'Digger.'

"Hurry up, Joe," shouted Tony. "It's our first dead drop. Jump in."

"Actually, Tony, I'm not feeling well today."

"Rubbish," replied Tony. "Get in. We're gonna earn today. We've got two pickups and deliveries."

"Yeah, hurry up, wimp. Did your mummy tell you not to play with bad boy, Tony?" Digger sniggered and beckoned me into the car.

"Now, Digger, I told you, leave Joe alone. We all have to learn, and Joe hasn't even started yet. Give him a break."

"Yeah, yeah," scoffed Digger. He leaned forward as I climbed into the front seat. "Here, Tony, what are we gonna call him?"

"You think of something, I've got better things to do," said Tony, steering the Cadi away from the curb.

"Where are we going," I asked, trying to sound casual. I was going to tell Tony I wanted out of his scheme but with Digger around - no way. The problem was if I took part I'd be guilty along with Tony and Digger.

"Now here's what's gonna' happen," continued Tony. "There's a disused warehouse on Nelson Street, down by the Grant High School playing field. At ten this morning, a waste truck is gonna' pull in and dump us a large package. They won't be stoppin' or talkin' to anyone and neither will we." He turned to me and out of the corner of his mouth, he said, "We don't know who they are and that's the way it has to be. Only the boss knows where they are comin' from and the boss he's doin' business with. So you wait until they pull out and back our truck, parked nearby, into the warehouse and pick up the parcel. When you've done that you call me and I'll tell you where to make the delivery. That clear?"

I nodded. My stomach was in knots, and I had an increasing urge to have a pee. What really frightened me was Tony's matter-of-fact way he described the job.

"So me and Digger are- "

"There's no 'me and Digger', Joe. You gotta' do the pick-up on your own."

My heart was pumping. Do the job on my own. Was Tony crazy? I'd never seen a dead body. I couldn't do it.

"I'll have the hole dug by the time you join us," chimed in Digger. "Don't want the bloody stiff layin' about, do we?"

The Cadi turned into Nelson Street. The place was deserted except for a vagrant crouched over in an empty office block entrance. I shivered and pulled the collar up on my jacket. An advertisement news sheet blown up from the gutter by a gusting breeze wrapped itself around my leg. I shrugged it off, wishing I could do the same with Tony's job.

The Cadi tail-light disappeared up the street as it began to rain. I found the warehouse, a large dilapidated, dirty

150

yellow brick building with one large double door covered in peeling white paint. Further on up the street was our truck. I climbed in just as a large refuge truck turned the corner.

I shivered again.

The refuge truck came past me and stopped a few yards the other side of the warehouse with a loud hiss of air-brakes. I slid down on my seat, keeping an eye on it through the wing mirror. One man jumped down from the cab and ran over to the warehouse double door with a key while the truck began reversing. It stopped as its rear end disappeared past the doors. Seconds later it drove back into the street and returned the way it had come.

"Damn it, that was slick," I said out loud, forgetting my immediate feelings and admiring these guys.

Don't get me wrong. Me and Tony spent three years running our neighborhood's booze and smokes business at night, and we had plenty of time stashing it, and us, away from the cops. We got good at that. But there's a big difference between what we were doing then and what Tony wants to do for his dad.

I turned the key in the ignition, and the engine coughed into life. The street was clear, and I didn't want to hang around. One minute later, I was looking at a roll of carpet taped up and sealed either end laying on a dirty floor littered with all sorts of rubbish.

The moment I picked one end of the carpet up, I puked.

Still gagging, I got one end of the carpet onto the pickup's tailboard and pushed the other end until I had it loaded. Without worrying about closing the doors, I left in a hurry and as soon as I got to the end of the street, called Tony.

"Well done, Joe. See, I told you it was a simple job, right?"

"Tony, I don't want to have anything to do with dead bodies. Can't we do the booze and other stuff?"

"First time's the worst time. After that it gets easy. Come on, Joe. You don't wanna' let me down, do you?"

"Well, no, but—"

"That's my buddy. Tell you what. When we finish today, let's go to 'Twinkles' that topless bar on sixth and Marsh Street. We'll celebrate and eat fried chicken. What d'ya say?"

"Yeah, I suppose." I didn't argue. The chicken at Twinkles was better than the meatloaf my mother had ready for dinner.

"Okay. We're at the railyard behind Saint Saviours graveyard. Get here as quick as you can. We need to get a move on if we wanna' make the other collection on time."

I drove as quick as I could. When I arrived, I realized I had not covered the carpet up with the tarpaulin neatly folded in one corner of the bed. The rain must have soaked it through. If there was any blood, it might get on our clothes. I reached the railyard and turned into the dirt track that led to the graveyard.

"Great timing. Digger just finished the hole." Tony helped

pull the carpet off. It was sealed both ends. "Don't worry ... no blood. Strangulation. One more then we can enjoy a night out at Twinkles."

Digger grinned. Twinkle ... your new name, Joe."

I didn't mind the nickname. Everyone had one. I guess even the dead guys had one. They were all called 'Stiff.'

"Here, grab hold the other end," wheezed Digger as he bent to pick up the carpet roll. "Drop him down the hole and help me cover him up."

Tony sat in the Cadi smoking while me and Digger filled the grave in and scattered some dust and rock over the top to hide the fresh dirt. It was Digger who really did all the work. He was a quiet giant of a man with muscular hairy arms. Even the backs of his hands were hairy across the knuckles. He had taken his jacket off and rolled up his shirt sleeves, revealing a tattoo of blood dripping from a dagger on one arm and a nude woman on the other. On the back of his neck, partially hidden beneath shoulder-length black hair, a thick white scar ran slantways across to his right shoulder. I did ask him once about it, and he told me that someone had cleavered him. His dark eyes narrowed as he had hissed -'so I stretched his neck like a chicken's.' Digger was a scary man, but he never argued, especially with Tony.

Tony, I learned later, was a Captain and Digger was a soldier. They were a strange couple, especially when together. At just five feet, Tony was dwarfed by his soldier who stood nearly seven feet tall and a lot broader. Both were always smartly dressed, but Digger wore a wide-brimmed trilby that made him look even more menacing.

"Come on then. Let's get going." Tony was impatient. "Give us five to clear before you move. Then go and wait for another delivery by the old college baseball stadium. Park in the far corner of the parking lot. An ice cream van will do the drop aways up from you. There's a clear patch of ground between two trees. Wait til he's gone before you pick up."

Digger stood behind him, leering at me. "Don't puke up this time Twinkle. You might get breakfast all over your sequined dress." He laughed.

Tony dug Digger in the ribs. "Concentrate and drive."

They climbed into the Cadi and drove off. I waited five minutes and followed. A short while later I entered the baseball stadium.

"Damn!" I thumped the steering wheel. An ice cream van was exiting and shot past me to join the highway.

It never occurred to me that the delivery might be early. Tony had arranged the drop so I guessed he would be real mad if something went wrong. I parked up and called him. I was right. He was mad.

"Go get the parcel, Joe, and meet Digger just inside that new complex their buildin' out on Interstate one fourty-six. There's a truck and trailer park there. He'll take you to the disposal point."

"We digging again?" I asked.

"Not this one, Joe. This guy's gettin' a concrete coffin."

The concrete coffin turned out to be the bottom of a foundation trench of a new warehouse being built behind a row of stores on an expanding shopping precinct.

Digger and I looked down at the grave site. "The trench is nice and deep," he said matter-of-factly. "We picked a spot where we can push the body under the water sealant sheeting, so we don't have to dig anything. Just a few shovels of shingle to cover him will do the trick. We have someone on the cementation crew. He's gonna' call the first cement truck to this position and start filling. No-one is gonna' know what's what."

We both stood looking down at the bottom of the trench. Worried about telling Tony I didn't want to do this kind of job anymore, I couldn't back out while I was with Digger.

The site was empty. It was lunchtime, and with the constant drizzle, workmen were gone for the day. It didn't take long to drop the carpet down and push it under the plastic sheet. When we were finished, there was nothing to be seen.

"Let's go and find Tony," I suggested. "I need to clean up."

Tony had a place of his own. His dad got it cheap, evidently on account of the fact that the realty company boss owed some favors after Mr. Sparizza had a chat with a friend in the D.A's office to make a charge of embezzlement go away. The apartment in one of the nicer suburbs of town was ideal for meetings and somewhere to clean up.

"Yeah, you gotta' look good for the girls, huh." Digger grinned. "Nothin' like a good night out after a good day's dig."

I turned the key, shuddering. The engine rattled into life.

***

"Okay, Twinkles it is, boys."

Tony walked into the room wearing a light blue suit with matching silk tie and highly polished ruby red crocodile shoes. Talk about a Hollywood star, he could have been a character from 'L.A. Confidential.' He stood posing in front of the mirror, adjusting his tie.

"Never mind the frickin' hairstyle, Elvis, how about some wedge?" scoffed Digger.

Tony turned, clicking his fingers. "Don't ever disrespect me like that again. You'll get your money when I'm ready."

Digger grunted, a mean look spreading across his face. His eyes narrowed, and I moved nearer the door as the two men squared up to one another.

"Listen, baby boy, your daddy might be the boss, but you're just a bad smell in daddy's shoes. Now, where's my wedge. We agreed a hundred a day."

"You ignorant punk, you think I'm where I am because my dad spoiled me? You insult the man who welcomed you to the family. That's too much, Digger."

My back was against the door as Digger lunged forward, his fists raised. I stepped between the men and fisted Digger's chest while grabbing his raised arm.

"No!" I screamed at Tony.

A shot rang out. Digger fell.

I stood, stunned at the sight of Digger lying on the carpet, a pool of blood gathering to one side of his body. Tony stood over him, shaking his head.

"He got what he deserved," he said through gritted teeth. "You don't disrespect a Captain like that. You gotta' remember that too, Joe."

I couldn't speak. I was too scared. My whole body was shaking, and I could only just hear Tony. His pistol shot was deafening. I just nodded, open-mouthed. It frightened me that Tony was so calm. He didn't care. His arm went around my shoulders, and I jumped.

"Tell you what, Joe. You go to Twinkles and meet the other two and send them back here. They can get rid of him." He bent forward and turning his head, looked up into my eyes. "You don't look too good, Joe. Go home after meeting them and get some zzzz's. You'll be okay."

"I don't want to be involved anymore, Tony." I was still shaking, and I quickly brushed a tear from my cheek. There was no way I was going to let Tony see me like that. I was scared, but I wasn't a pussy.

"Joe, come on. I know this is the first time you've seen

the makin' of a stiff, but once you've seen one, you've seen them all. You'll get used to it, stop worryin' yourself." He put an arm around me and walked me to the door. "Now go see the boys at Twinkles and get a drink while you're there. Tell Kinky, the owner, to put you on my tab.

A half hour later I was sitting at the bar in Twinkles trying to figure things. I could understand someone getting wasted for murder, rape, or even stealing but for insulting someone, even if it were a Captain. It just didn't make sense to me. This setup just wasn't for me. I had to get away. If the cops knew there was a killing and who the dead man was, the Feds would be all over the place.

"Call for you, Joe." Fingers, the barman, tossed me his cell and flicked a towel over the counter where ash from the cigarette drooping from his mouth had fallen.

I looked at the screen. It was my mother. "Say, hi mom." I tried to sound matter-of-fact but failed miserably.

"What the hell of you got yourself into?" she demanded. "I've had cops around here asking to see you."

My heart thumped. Both hands started shaking again. "What about?"

"Stolen whiskey and cigarettes. I don't have to ask if Tony was involved."

I breathed deeply with relief. "Nothing to do with me. Stop worrying mom. I'll sort things out."

The phone rang again as I finished the call. It was Tony.

"Yeah, Joe, I've taken care of it. The boys have cleaned

up, and Digger's been packaged. We'll take him for a ride to the coast tomorrow, and he can have a nice sea trip."

Fingers sucked on a toothpick and watched me stagger from the bar.

The rain was falling again. I didn't care. My jacket was soaked in seconds, and my feet squelched as water seeped through the bottom of my trainers. I stood on the edge of the curb and breathed in lungfuls of air. An old Chrysler driven by some black dude went past at speed sending a sheet of dirty water over my jeans. As the car disappeared up the street, I saw through the rear window an apologetic hand raised. So what? I didn't give him a thought. In fact, I didn't give anybody a thought. My head was so mixed up I wanted to puke, laugh, and cry all at the same time.

Tony was wise-cracking and laughing when he called. It didn't bother him that he had killed Digger. Maybe he was a phsyco, I don't know, but all I could think of at that moment was the shooting and all the blood. As I stood in the rain, my head cleared a little, and I decided to go see Mr. Sparizza and tell him I wanted out. After all, I wasn't a 'made' man.

My heart was in my mouth as I rang the bell at the Sparizza mansion.

"You see, Sir," I explained a moment later, "I'm not cut out for killing and burying. Tony's great at it but not me. I'd rather deal with the cigarettes and whiskey. That's what I'm good at." I smiled, but the smile was false and evaporated quickly.

"Well now, Joe. What you're going through is under-standable." Sparizza did the same as his son and put an arm around my shoulders.

I wasn't all that keen on that. I'd seen things like that in the movies. You know - when a boss wants to get rid of someone, he always smiles and acts nice to the guy being bumped off and puts an arm around the victim.

"Tell you what, Joe. Look after Tony for two more jobs, and if you still feel the same, then I'll put you back on the cigarettes and whiskey. Maybe I'll let you go solo and take charge of that end of things. Whatdya say, huh?"

I didn't want to let Tony down, and I'd have a chance of running the booze on my own. It was a way out. At least I wouldn't have to deal with stiffs.

I nodded agreement and left feeling relieved.

***

It was an old red shrimper, the top of its rusting wheel-house just visible above the quayside. Tony and I looked down at the untidy mass of ropes, chains, and piled fishing nets that littered her deck.

"Okay, let's heave Digger down there onto the deck. The crew will arrive soon, and we don't wanna' be here then."

Digger was rolled up in a sealed carpet like the others. We pulled him off the pickup and threw him over the quay and onto the boat.

"Hold it! What's in that rug?"

Two cops stepped from behind a crate, guns drawn.

***

"We know all about the Whiskey, Joe ... and cigarettes. Your name's been on my wall for months but I kind of thought you might snitch for me when I had more on you so you and I could do a deal."

The cop who introduced himself as Lieutenant Schriver looked at me through the driving mirror as we turned slowly from the lot.

"I hear Tony's a big shot for daddy. How about you, Joe? Now you've had a chance to see what's going on it's time you got out while you can walk, isn't it?"

Tony said nothing, neither did I. I guessed it was better for me to stay firmly zipped up. The Lieutenant looked sideways. "Hey, Bruce, what d'ya say we take them to the precinct warehouse and soften them up a little?"

Bruce, a heavyset man wearing a trilby and open raincoat, replied gruffly. "Yeah, only this time don't get over enthusiastic. I ain't gonna cover for you on another broken jaw."

I looked at Tony, and he smiled.

"Don't worry, Joe. These two dicks 'ain't gonna' do anythin'. They ain't got nothin' but heavy rocks between their ears." Tony leaned forward. "I want our lawyer. Till then we ain't sayin' nothin' to you. I'm takin' the fifth."

The detectives burst into loud laughter. The patrol car swerved around a corner and pulled into a parking lot near the warehouse I had collected the first stiff from. They got out of the car and pulled me roughly from the back. A black hood suddenly slid over my head, blotting out Schriver's smirking face.

"Okay smartass, let's take a walk. You're on your own. Tony 'Baby-Face,' has got a room all his own."

I stumbled forward across the concrete, my hands cuffed and held by Schriver to guide me.

We walked slowly through a door, and I got pushed into a chair. My body and legs were tied down, and that's when I got the shivers. If they were going to work me over, I'd try staying quiet.

"Okay, Joe, spill or be given the water treatment."

Cold water poured over my head, and I couldn't help it. Damn it. I screamed.

"We know you were actively involved in Digger's death, Joe. Tell us about Tony doing him, or I'll pin this job onto you."

"I ain't no snitch," I screamed. "I don't know anything about murder. It wasn't Tony. He's innocent. Go to hell."

I heard someone snigger, and then a load of water was poured over my head again. I screamed, but at the same time, there was a lot of laughter.

The hood came off my head, and all the boys and Mr. Sparizza were gathered around me.

"Sorry to play this on you, Joe. It was Tony's idea. He wanted you to be a 'made' man, so I wanted to make sure of your loyalty."

The short ceremony followed, and the first guy to hug me was Digger. He turned out to be a real friend.

Little did any of us know what was going to happen next.

And little did I know on the day I had my thumb cut and had a piece of card burn in the palm of my hand that my life as a 'gopher' would end. I would become a vital and much-needed cog in the mob's well-oiled machine. My rise to fame started with a business idea a few months later, inspired by the boys. After Tony had given his blessing, he arranged a meeting with his father for me. Mr. Sparizza loved my idea and funded me, although he insisted on forty percent interest plus a cut from my profits. I guess that was right. I didn't argue anyway. A year later I married my Clare and a few months after that along came a son.

Every morning I dressed in a suit and left for the office with a briefcase. All in all, I lived the typical American dream. I told my wife I was running an insurance office and we were doing well, and that's how it's been for the last twenty years.

***

The first cut was a disaster. My tutor had a good laugh as the pig's intestines spilled out onto the floor, clogging up the metal grid above the long channel drain that carried blood into a tank buried under the floor.

"You won't get your certificate if you do that in front of the inspectors," laughed George Stanton.

Stanton was a master butcher, and after being offered ten grand, he agreed to teach me butchery. I spent a year until I could not only butcher carcasses but could cut beef and pork limbs as well as all the cuts sold in supermarkets. After eighteen months I was fully trained and received a certificate. My parents were proud of me but couldn't understand how my qualification had anything to do with the mob. Two months later the boss bought me an abattoir on the outskirts of town and through his protection business, got all the local meat markets, butchers, and fast food outlets to order their meat from me. Trade was fantastic.

**

It was on a Friday a year later, and I was just about done when the phone rang. It was the boss.

"Joe, sorry to put this one on you but I have a rush job. You'll get delivery in about an hour. Get it finished and loaded on a trolley and stick it in the freezer. It'll be picked up around two a.m."

You never disrespect the boss, ever. You get the job done.

I agreed and called Clare to tell her I'd be late home from the office. Sure enough, a truck I recognized as one of our own arrived. A long canvas bag was placed on a trolly while I opened up and switched on the cutting line I kept empty for specialized jobs.

I pushed the trolly to the end of the line and opened it, mumblin' to myself as I often did.

"Twinkle, twinkle little star,

Cops are wondrin' where you are.

In the sea or under mud,

All that's left is pools of blood."

My heart thumped. Of all the stiffs I had cut since starting the business this was one I never expected to see. It was Digger.

Strange, but he was the only corpse I had any feelings for as I cut off his head.

FIREFLY

If something seems too good to be true, then it usually isn't. More often than not, we end up learning a lesson by getting our fingers burned, vowing not to get into that deal or situation again. But what if that ' too good to be true' turned out to be true even though the law had to be broken? Would you still go for it - and would you do it again if the reward was hard to resist?

Out of work and with nothing to lose except maybe his freedom, our chancer makes a decision that could well change his fortunes.

I watched the big Georgian house on the corner of Marcus and 22nd street. Number 3275 was in darkness. The upper window panes reflected dancing orange light from a street lamp masked by two large Mountain Ashes waving furiously in the gusty wind. A looping telephone cable slapped rhythmically against the flagpole in the front garden. In the middle of the driveway a rolled newspaper in a polythene sheath, that day's headline still unread, slid sideways and got stuck in a large puddle.

A woman's distinctive baritone voice, rising above the noisy elements, came from a house down the street a-ways.

"Say Claude; don't forget to put the trash at the end of the drive. You know what them guys are like. They'll tip shit all over the lawn if you don't put it at the end of the drive."

I turned my head and watched a small black guy waddle down his driveway and dump a couple of trash bags on the sidewalk, shaking his hand as though dismissing the irritating voice. He turned to face the direction the order came from.

"Missus, you better shut that mouth of yours," he shouted, "or I swear I'm gonna' get em to take you away too."

I pulled the hood closer around my head and looked down at my feet where a piece of paper had wrapped itself around one foot and flapped madly in the wind. I reached down and picked the paper up.

It was an official auction notice for the sale of 3275, 22nd street. The county was selling the house against the unpaid property tax.

I crumpled the notice up and threw it away, smiling.

It was damn cold. My eyes watered and my nose and ears stung. Rain and sleet threatened, but that wouldn't be until the morning. For the time being, the gusty wind was playing havoc with anything that moved, whistling through trees and rattling windows as the people of Milford Heights began to sleep through a restless night. A police siren wailed in the distance. It was to late to back out now. The old girl was paying good money. I thought back to my conversation with her and hoped she would be pleased with the results and I'd receive the balance of the fee she offered.

***

A fluorescent buzzed and flickered in the middle of the restaurant ceiling. Making it hard to read the small print in the paper.

I propped the Post up against the sugar shaker and read the advert a second time while forking fried egg and grits. The job seemed too good and easy to be true. I wondered if the advertiser was genuine or just playing a joke. Above the front counter chatter, the TV, and the noisy hissing A/C unit in the corner of the diner a soft southern voice sounded in my ear, disturbing my train of thought.

"You want more coffee, honey bee? I got plenty in the pot."

Without looking up, I pointed my fork at the mug. An anonymous hand sporting two large rings and a silver charm bracelet dangling from the wrist appeared in front of me. As the coffee pot was tipped, the bracelet clacked against the glass. The aroma was strong and inviting.

Wiping my mouth on a napkin, I sipped the coffee before deciding to make a call to the number listed and apply for the job. After all, what did I have to lose? The money was good, and I needed to do more than live on a Social check. At thirty-three, I wasn't going to spend my life on the streets.

The advert didn't say too much except it was a one-off job and paid five hundred bucks. Only a strong young guy need apply. Out of work for a year since the mill closed down and with no other prospects, I wanted in.

Ten minutes later, avoiding the puddles of rainwater in muddy dips created by trucks, I walked across the dirt parking lot outside Jenny's to the telephone stand. I put my hand to one ear as an eighteen wheeler spewing diesel fumes passed close by along the highway. Coughing on the fumes, I placed my last quarter in the slot and stabbed the number on the worn keypad.

The line was dead for a few seconds, and then I heard the far-off gentle ringtone. There was a click. A female voice I guessed well into old age answered.

"You ring about the job?"

"Yes, ma'am."

"You seen the inside of a cell?"

"No, ma'am."

"Single?"

"Yes, ma'am."

"Been in the military?"

"Yes, ma'am."

About twenty questions later she surprised me and said I had the job and to expect a letter in the post containing instructions on what she needed doing. She didn't want to tell me what the situation was about over the phone and the details I should keep to myself. Half the money was included inside the letter and the other half would be wired on completion of the job.

I kept thinking about her last question which intrigued me. Would I like to be famous and could I keep a secret? I guessed she might be a bit cranky and put it out of my mind. She was certainly trusting, sending half the money although, despite that, her cracked shrill voice came over stern – like a school mistress.

The address I gave the woman was a flop on the outskirts of Milford owned by 'Smitty,' an old friend of mine from Nam. He'd been divorced several years and let me crash out for a few months. Money was scarce, so we ate whenever we got really hungry but smoked and drank most days. It was an existence I loathed but one that 'Smitty' had accepted as his lot.

Three days later the letter arrived and the money with it. The instructions were clear and concise, but I wondered what my employer's reasons were for doing such a thing. I'd find out about her intentions in the newspapers later, she wrote.

I thought about it for a while and figured I could walk away with the two hundred and fifty bucks, but something besides the rest of the money made me decide I'd go through with the job. Maybe it was because I was dealing with a lady, who knows.

I had plenty of time to do the job so I got Smitty to walk across town with me to the smarter suburb where money lived and where I was to carry out the task.

The area was beautiful: trimmed hedges and manicured lawns that sloped down to the edge of clean sidewalks free of weeds poking out of cracked pavements. It smelled nice too.

My instructions said no-one was at home and after twelve at night the whole street was asleep. Residents here were middle to old age; retired couples, their educated kids all married and gone to work for Bill Gates.

I found the address and took a good look at the house. The driveway and front garden was as she had described it.

'Go onto the driveway and cut across the lawn. The trees will hide you until you reach the side entrance. The door has a glass panel to the top, and this is the way in. There is no burglar alarm.'

The following day I had a shopping list she had sent me and bought the items listed one at a time from different shops and paid cash as instructed.

When I got back to Smitty's, I sat in his garage for an hour shaping a small hollow in one side of the balsa wood block and preparing the rest of the materials. I sat thinking about something else the old lady had said; that if all went well, she would recommend me to friends. It was a strange remark, to say the least, but hell, five hundred bucks not only bought my agreement to accept the job but my silence too without trying to understand her motives.

'It glows for as long as you want, depending on the length of the fuse cord. The tip smolders red. When the fuse burns down to the top edge of the ping pong ball stuck in the balsa wood, it drops down inside the hole and into the lighter fluid. For a few seconds, the light plastic ball will get brighter and brighter until melting plastic allows the burning liquid to spread across the balsa wood.'

All this she explained in neatly handwritten instructions.

'The balsa wood burns easily and ignites the pile of crumpled paper you have placed on the floor beneath the window. Make sure you open the window a crack. As the fire from the paper spreads, the draft from the window will fan the flames which will then ignite the curtains. Setting everything up at the back in the living room will hide the fire until it is too late.'

***

The biting cold wind was making my eyes water. I wanted to walk away, to get far away from the house but I had to make sure things were going according to plan.

'By now the paper should be alight,' I thought. 'Another couple of minutes and the room will be engulfed. Where the bloody hell is the smoke?

It was five minutes before I saw a few red sparks spiralling almost sideways from the rear of the house.

I shivered and walked to the end of Marcus and turned right into McDonalds before I heard the wail of a siren. As I ordered a coffee, two fire trucks raced past to the fire.

The papers quoted the fire chief the following day. The house burned to the ground, and nothing indicated arson. The probable cause of the fire, an electrical fault.

Two days later Smitty woke me. "You got mail," he called. "Get your ass down here; it looks like Fargo sent you some dough."

Sure enough, it was and with it another letter from a PO Box in Texas.

'As my apprentice, you succeeded admirably, and I want to congratulate you. Should you decide to make this your new career, please ring the enclosed telephone number for your next job. I will contact you as each new client contacts me. Yours, Firefly.'

THE BANSHEE AND THE RAVEN

My wife, Mrellan, wrote this story several years before she passed away. She had always meant to rework the story but never got around to completing it. What sets it aside is the writing style; it pulls the reader into an unusual tale with great descriptive work. The lack of editing almost pales into insignificance. I love this Irish fairy fantasy.

This is an unedited draft.

The last echo of the banshee's wail faded as a raven took wing and flew across the face of the full moon. An old woman's moon, the country folk called it. They said the full moon was a wise, old woman, and God help the man who laughed at her, for she would curse the rest of his days with misery. They said the next day the neighbors came to check on the old woman and she was not there. They said nobody ever saw the old woman again. For weeks a great raven, so black that it shone blue in the sunlight, sat on the lantern hook by the front door. They said the old woman was a witch and when she died, she turned into that raven. The old Irish folk tales still live, and strange things happened out on the Connemara.

***

Sure as I know, my Christian name is Margaret Mary, between the howling of the wind of the ocean, on that cold, clear March night, I heard the banshee wail for the first time. Ma'am said I listened to too many stories and believed the silly old songs sung around the fire in the wintertime. Nevertheless, I know what I heard. I would have known even if no one told me. It was a death wail.

Everyone who knew the old woman either feared or cursed her. Heathen was what they called her. She didn't have a Christian name. Her name came from the old Celts and the fairy folk they said.

Ytha is what she told me to call her that first day I saw her. I was playing hide and seek with the old herding dog down the lane. I climbed the wee stonewall to see where the dog had gone. When I looked up, there she was.

She wasn't near as tall as ma'am, all bent over with a heavy black shawl wrapped around her head and shoulders. Her black skirt was ratted and ragged at the edges. Her shoes were so old that they were not even black anymore. Her hair was gray and matted like it was rarely brushed. But the thing I really noticed was her eyes. I never saw eyes like that before. They were a ghostly color of white-gray, like no color at all. Ma'am said she was blind. I've never been around someone who was blind.

When I came over the wall, she just stood there, about three foot away from me. Her face turned in my direction, but I knew she didn't see me. Somehow, I knew right away she couldn't see. Her nose twitched, as a rabbit does when it senses danger. She was leaning on an old tree branch that was almost as twisted and Bent as she was. I froze when I saw her; she was the most fearsome thing I had ever seen. I just knew she was a fairy witch and I was going to get a curse on my head. Her voice sounded like a rusty hinge on the big oak front door.

"Who's there? Speak up I say, who's there?

The dog barked. I was so scared. I fell off the wall and landed on a pile at her feet. I picked myself up, fast as I could, and answered her in a squeaky little voice that didn't even sound like me.

"Tis I, Margaret Mary O'Halloran. I live down the lane, and I was just playing with the dog.

The dog barked again as if confirming what I told the old woman.

"Well, if you must be here, come in and help me make

tea. You can slice the brack for me.

I just stood there staring at her. Somehow she knew that.

"What are you looking at child?" she asked in a voice that didn't seem so raspy now

"They all say you are a fairy witch. Is that true?"

She just snorted as she turned around and started feeling her way back to the cottage. "Believe anything you hear do ya? Don't be a fool. Let's get out of this wind before it cuts ya to bits."

The one-room cottage wasn't near as big as my ma'am's kitchen and parlor.

Once whitewashed walls were now gray-streaked from coal and peat that burned continuously in the little hearth at the far end. A hand-made rocking chair sat to one side of the hearth. A little cot, covered with a dingy sheet and coarse wool blanket hugged the wall. Her clothes hung on a roughly carved peg, hammered into the wall above the bed. At the other end of the room was a small sideboard, a table with a plain chair and a three-legged stool. She shuffled around the room putting the teapot on the hook, in the hearth and getting dishes and a loaf of brown raisin brack out of the sideboard.

She picked up a cracked and crazed teapot from the dry sink and threw in a handful of tea, from a box, which had a faded picture of biscuits on it. "Don't just stand there staring," she said impatiently. "Slice that brack and spread it with that butter in that tub."

I couldn't get over the fact that although she was stone blind, she knew my every move, even when I was just standing and staring. The kettle over the fire began steaming, and she took the edge of her skirt and fetched it off the hook.

The smell of tea and peat filled the room as she sat in her rocking chair, she munched on the brack and took great slurps of the strong, black tea. A shaft of sunlight streaked across the room from one of the two windows. I watched hen feathers zigzag down from the roosting basket hanging in the rafters as I chewed the dry brack. Maam would have thrown it out to the pigs rather than giving it to us. Even the raisins were tough and hard. The tea tasted strong and bitter, and I wished I had some milk in it. I was too scared to ask the old woman for milk, or sugar either, and she didn't offer. Maybe she was too poor to have any long twisted strands, I thought.

It seemed she had forgotten I was even there as she stared into the fire with those horrible unseeing eyes. I wished I could leave, but I didn't know how to do it and be polite. Suddenly she coughed; it was a great, loud, wet noise. She brushed long twisted strands of hair away from her face and turned to me. "Be a love and pour me some more tea, child. These old bones pain me terribly every time I stand."

I jumped up, and my foot caught the edge of the chair and tipped it over.

"You sure are a clumsy child. Just like a calf who aren't

used to being in a stall. See if you can pour that tea without breaking the pot." She grumbled at me, but I could see just a hint of a smile around the edges of her mouth.

"Yes ma'am," I said, being very careful as I poured the tea. Her hand brushed against mine as she took the cup back. It felt cold and rough. I reached into the old wooden box by the chair to get turf for the fire, but the box was empty.

"Would you like me to bring in some turves for you? The box is empty, and the coal bucket is almost empty."

Yellow, broken teeth showed through the smile that was higher on one side of her face. "Bless you, child, I would like that. It is so cold, the wind makes even this ugly old face hurt."

It took several trips, but I filled the box with turves. By the time the coal bucket was full, the sun was already sinking back into the choppy gray waters of the Atlantic. The stone fences in the field between the cottage and the bay cast black shadows that crisscrossed like giant tic-tac-toe games.

"I guess I best get headed for home before my Maam starts worrying about me. Thanks for the tea and brack," I said with my best Sunday manners. She didn't hear me though. Her head drooped between her hunched shoulders, and the rhythmic sound of her weasy breath told me she was asleep.

The next day was Sunday. After Mass, we all piled into

Da's little car and went to Gran's for dinner. It was dark when we came home. Da had to drive by the old thatch to get to our place, and I saw the fire light dimly shining from the window. When I said my prayers that night, I silently asked God to take care of the old lady, even if she was a witch. I was sure that God loved witches as much as he loves good Catholic girls.

Monday after school I ran all the way home, changed out of my uniform before ma'am told me to, and fed the chickens.

"Maam, I did my chores. Can I go play now?" I yelled through the open door.

"Margaret Mary, what has gotten into you today? Are you sure you're done? It usually takes twice this long to do your chores."

"I'm all done Maam. Can I go play now?" I said impatiently, wanting to be off across the rocky field.

'All right, but be home before dusk. There is a storm brewing, and I don't want you out in it. And don't forget your cap and scarf."

"Yes, Maam."

I could see smoke curling out of the chimney when I climbed over the stonewall. I stepped over a skinny, orange tomcat and knocked on the door.

The old woman opened the door with one hand and grabbed her shawl around her with the other. "Who is it?" she crackled, "and what do you want?"

I wondered what had possessed me to want to see her, "Tis Margaret Mary. I came to see how you are."

"Tis more likely you came to eat the rest of my brack! she said. "Come in if you must, but I've already had my tea, and the cat ate the last crumbs of brack. It was stale anyway."

She shuffled over to her chair and fell into it with a grunt.

"Throw a handful of coal on the fire and pull up that stool. No sense in being cold when I pay that outrageous price for coal."

She just sat in her chair and rocked for the longest time, her face turned to the hearth to get every bit of warmth the coal would give.

'So why did you come?" Children are usually afraid of me and stay away. I think you are too, but you came anyway. Why. What do you want of me?"

"I don't know," I said, afraid to lie. I knew if I lied, she would know. Maam always did. I swallowed hard and went on. "I don't believe you are a mean, old witch. I came to see how you are and to talk to you, I guess."

"I'm a blind old woman, the cold makes my bones hurt, and the smoke from the coal makes it hard to breathe. I feel terrible, and I am miserable! Even the cat would rather be outside than sit in my lap these days. So if that is all you wanted to know maybe you should just go home." Her shaking hands rearranged her shawl. A grimace crossed her face as if even this small motion caused her pain.

I didn't move, mainly because of fear, I guess, but something inside me said, she's just a sad old woman. My heart reached out to her. Her next words scared me, and I jumped.

"Don't feel sorry for me, you foolish girl! If you really do care, fill that turf box, so that I don't have to." Her voice softened a little.

I filled the box and checked the coal bucket, and then sat back down on the three-legged stool, and tucked my feet under it. Resting my chin on my upturned hands, I stared into the fire.

"Fires have great magic, you know," said the old woman. This time it did not scare me that she could read my thoughts.

"When I could see, that was one of the things I loved most to watch. I still love to watch the flames, but now I have to look with my heart."

I could see the reflection of the flames on her face and I understood what she was saying.

I stared into the flame. "What is so magical about a fire?" I asked, not really believing her, but hoping that she was right.

"No magic is going to work unless you believe in it," said Ytha. "The first rule of magic is: magic is only as powerful as you believe it is. But then you are a good Catholic girl, so you don't believe anything I say anyway."

I didn't know what to say, so I changed the subject, "Have

you always lived here?"

"No, not always," she said. Her hands relaxed in her lap and the tension left her face. "I once lived in town. That was back in the days when they believed I was useful. Back before I got old, and the children called me a witch. People respected me then. I was the town midwife."

Her voice had that far away sound that all grown-ups get when they talk about the old days. As she stared unseeing into the flames, her voice lowered almost to a whisper. I scooted my stool closer to hear the old woman's tale.

***

'Back then, I birthed most of the babies here about. I had a little carriage and a sturdy gray poney, and I even went out into the wilds of the Connemara. Once I was called to birth a baby not too far from her. I had been to that house three times before but still there had never been a bairn in the crib by the fire. Always, the babies died in a few hours after birthin'. The young couple seemed so loving and kind. I wondered what they did to displease the gods so.

I wanted to cry when that bairn came out. That child too had the curse upon it. The mother knew as soon as she held her. She was so tiny and fragile. Her lips were the blue of a baby bewitched with the chill of the soul. It broke my heart to see the tears run down the mother's face and she begged me to do something for the child.

186

That evening when I was sitting by my fire, I heard a wee voice singing. Right out of the flames, stepped a fairy. He wasn't much taller than that stool you're sitting on. He was dressed in a fine brown suit with a belt of gold holding the jacket closed. A matching cock hat tipped to one side over his ear, and he had bright gold buckles on his shoes. He just stood on the hearth just looking at me for the longest time. When he spoke, he said he knew about the baby I birthed that day. Now I know that a fairy never does nothing without getting paid for it.

"What is your price sir?" I asked.

'I ask only the usual payment," he replied, with a self-satisfied smirk. "I must have the bairn to raise as my own. You will tell the parents that the child is dead."

I told him no. I told him how the parents already lost three babies, and I feared that the young mother's heart could not bear the loss of another. The fairy just looked at me and kept smiling. "Would you be willing to pay the ransom for the child?"

"Ask what you will, and I will consider it. I say."

The fairy tapped his foot and scratched his head for a minute, and then he says, "I will give you the child's life if you give me your eye-sight."

Now that shocked me so much I didn't know what to say. "You have one day to think about it," he said. "I will be back tomorrow night for your answer. " With that, he jumped into the air and disappeared.

187

The next day I visited the mother and child. The child was worse. She quaked as if her very soul was frozen, and her breath came in little gasps. She would not nurse, and she was even too weak to cry. Her mother held her in one arm and counted the beads of a rosary with the other. I knew her prayers would not work.

That night I told the fairy I would accept his offer. "you would do that for someone who isn't even kin?" he asked in amazement. "Why?"

"Because I know the heartbreak of never having a child," I told him.

'Yes, so do I," he said. "All the women in my clan are barren. There have been no babies for many years. That is why I wanted this one. It is fairy law that I give you a chance to bargain. I will accept your eyesight as a ransom for the child. You will not go blind until one year from this day. On that night I will visit you and take you sight." Then he disappeared.

The child, of course, lived and grew to be a healthy and beautiful girl. Her parents worshipped her, and she was the joy of their life.

A few months later, I moved into this cottage. The fairy returned as he promised, but before he took my sight, he told me that his clan had been so impressed with my love that they had offered to help me by teaching me the herb craft and helping me begin my garden. That garden served me well for many years. They must have put an enchantment on it because the plants grew and bloomed all year round. Even at Christmas, I could pick fresh dill, rosemary, thyme, and mint. Folks thought I grew my plants inside, but I never did.

For some years, I would load up my buggy every Saturday, hitch up the pony, go into the town market, and sell my wares.I always carried my medicine box and put it under the counter of my booth. It contained the special herbs and potions that the wee folk taught me to make for ailing children. I gave mothers with babes a lot of croup tea in those days.

Then one Saturday, in the spring, I was coming home, and I heard some young boys yelling and calling me names. They threw stones at the pony and me. The pony panicked and ran into the ditch. It broke its leg, and the cart turned over on me. Your own Da found me and brought me home. I was hurt bad, and what with arthritis I never got out again. How was I to go out? My pony was shot, and the cart was in bits.

For these past few years, the wee folk is the only ones who cared for or visited me. Even the tinkers stay away from my door. That is 'til you and that infernal dog decided to climb my fence.'

The old woman sighed deeply, wrapped her knurled fingers around the arms of her chair, and forced herself to her feet. "It must be getting on toward dark now. You better get home before your Maam starts worrying about you," she said, Bending to put more coal on the little fire grate. "Tomorrow I'm making fresh brack, so I suppose you'll want to come and get your share."

"Thank you, Maam. I'll come if I can," I wrapped my scarf around my neck and pulled the wool cap down over my ears. I could hear the wind whistling threw the little stonewall across the field, even before I opened the door.

The next day Maam had company for tea and she hardly even noticed when I asked to go outside. She only repeated her instruction that I wear my cap and scarf.

I could smell the freshly baked brack as I knocked on the old woman's door. She opened the door with a big grin on her haggard old face. "Ah, sure as flowers bloom in the spring, I knew you couldn't resist the smell of sweet bread cooking. Come in, come in, child."

That afternoon, as we sipped tea and ate the bread, she told me more stories about how she had delivered most of the babies in County Galway.

My Da is from a family of ten children. Old Ytha had brought most of them into the world. She told me people paid her with jars of jam and pots of thick, brown stew. I loved to sit by the fire and listen to her stories, but she always seemed to know when it was nigh on to sunset, and she would chase me out the door just before the first stars appeared.

For the rest of that winter, I went down to old Ytha's cottage every chance I got. One afternoon, a week after Patty's

Day, I climbed over the wall and didn't see any smoke coming from her chimney. I thought that was strange because it was still cold enough for me to wear my heavy jacket outside. I knocked on her door and heard no answer. I got scared that something had happened to the old woman. I ran all the way back to my mama's kitchen.

"Maam, you have to help me," I said between gasps of air. "The old woman down the way, Ytha, she won't answer her door, and there's no smoke coming out of her chimney. Maam, she must be sick or hurt! We have to find out."

"Calm down, child. When your Da comes home, I'll have him go check on her. Now hang your coat on the peg and set the table for me." She calmly went about fixing the dinner without another word about the matter.

I knew not to argue with her. Da always says Ma'am is the stubbornist woman he ever knew.

Soon as Da's car pulled up in the driveway, I shot out the front door to tell him.

"Well now what is all this fuss," he asked, holding out his arms to catch me and give me a hug.

'Da, I think old Ytha is sick or hurt. She won't answer her door, and there's no smoke from her chimney. Maam says you would go down and see. Can I come with you Da? She is my friend."

"Now, now," he said, opening the front door and motioning me to go in first. "Let me kiss your Maam before I have her mad at me. I'll go down and check on Ytha, but I think you should stay here and help your mama get dinner ready."

It seemed as if Da was gone a very long time and when he came through the back door, his face was real serious, like when his sister got hurt in a motor accident. He didn't say anything to either Maam or me. He just walked over to the phone and dialed a number.

"Dr. O'Flaherty, this is Ullick O'Halloran, out at Boley Beg. Could you come out and look at Ytha-the old woman who lives down the lane from me. She appears to be pretty ill."

A little while later, the doctor's black Rover pulled through our gate and parked behind Da's car.

"You stay here, Margaret Mary, give the doctor a chance to examine the old woman." I watched the light from their torches bob up and down as they crossed the field with its great ghostly rocks and shadowy fences. I crossed myself and silently asked God to make Ytha better.

They didn't come back until I took my bath and put on my fuzzy, flannel nightdress. Maam said I could sit in the parlor and wait for Da and Dr. O'Flaherty. When Da came back, Maam met him at the door, and I could hear them talking low, in the entry. Like they didn't want me to hear what they were saying. Da came into the parlor, sat down beside me, and put his arm around me. "Margaret Mary, Ytha is very, very sick. The doctor says she may not live much longer."

I felt the tears burn in my eyes and roll down my cheeks. "Oh, Da!" was all I could say. He hugged me while I cried for the strange old woman. After a few minutes, he wiped my tears with his handkerchief and told me I could go see her after school the next day.

I ran all the way home from school and Maam met me at the door. She already had her coat on, and she held a soup pot wrapped in a towel. "I'm taking this soup down to Ytha. Please get the loaf of bread from the kitchen counter."

The old woman looked so pale lying on her cot. More like a shadow than the feisty old lady who somehow knew what I was doing whenever I was in her cottage. I sat on the edge of her bed, my fingers playing with the hem of her blanket.

"Quit fidgeting child," said the old woman, in a weak voice that didn't even try to sound mean. "And stop those tears. Death ain't nothing to cry about. It's as natural as birthin', I don't know why they cry at death. Death is better than life for me now. I have lived a long life, and now I will soon be under the hill with the fairies. Be happy for my child. I will once again see the moon and dance by the bonfire."

I sniffed and wiped my eyes with the back of my hand. "But I won't see you anymore, and I will miss you terribly."

Her shriveled hand reached from under the covers and found mine. She squeezed it, and her voice lowered to a soft murmur. I Bent down to hear her, "When you see the Raven, smile, for 'tis an enchantment by the wee folk, and know that it is a friend."

Maam shooed me out of the cottage. She said Ytha need-ed her peace. Before I left, I Bent down and kissed the old woman's cheek, knowing that I would never see her again.

Later that evening when Maam put our dinner on the ta-ble, I saw a tear run down her cheek. "Maam, why are you crying?" I asked.

She turned away and stood at the sink looking out to-ward the old woman's cottage. "Ytha was a midwife. My mama always swore, if it had not been for Ytha I would have died. The old folks say that I was born with the chill of the soul. I couldn't breathe or keep my body warm. My Maam lost three children before I was born and another one after me. Everyone swore that it was old Ytha and her potions that kept me alive."

During the middle of that night, I woke to the sound of the banshee's wail. I sat straight up in my bed and wrapped my blanket around my arms. The full moon shone threw my window. As I sat there, thinking about Ytha, I saw the raven fly across the moon. I smiled, crossed myself, and thanked God for Ytha. Then I snuggled down in my com-forter and went back to sleep.

The Inspiration that led to Little Gems

LITTLE GEMS is a collection of short stories that have been inspired by Ray's involvement with **The Story Mint**, a New Zealand writing organization for aspiring writers that boasts a worldwide membership.

Ray was instrumental in helping to start The Story Mint's unique serial writing project. These serials, each written by ten separate authors from across the globe, have become popular and have helped new and experienced writers showcase their work.

Several stories in LITTLE GEMS first appeared as "One Author" serials written by Ray Stone for The Story Mint.

https://www.thestorymint.com/

About Ray Stone

Ray is an accomplished author with a variety of published works to his name.

Born just outside London in 1946, he grew up in post war Britain during a period of depression and ration books, bombed out housing and BBC radio. At school he won a writing competition at the age of eleven and later in his teens went on to widen his interest in the arts.

At the age of eighteen, Ray began writing poetry and lyrics whilst studying at college.

During the following years, he worked in theatre as a technician with many orchestras and artists including the London Philharmonic, London Symphony, Mantovani, The original Doyle Carte Opera Company, Harlequin Ballet, Joan Baez, Jimmy Hendrix, Oscar Peterson and worked on local shows such as *My Fair Lady, Camelot* and *West Side Story*.

His poetry won him first place in a 1998 international internet poetry competition with 'Angry Silence.' Moving to Colchester in the same year, he wrote a full page article about the historical significance of the locale and was published with a by-line in the local press.

Whilst writing his first novel Ray returned to writing lyrics and teamed up with a local composer. Together they produced and recorded five blues numbers.

In England, Ray lived in and around London's colourful East End and the café sets of Westminster and Kensington. Through rubbing shoulders with the rich and famous — and infamous — he has acquired a unique insight into the lives of both criminal and upper classes that give his works a believable realism.

Ray moved to the USA in 2003 and has since retired from a successful landscape design business. He now lives in Cyprus, where he continues to write and publish. He is also an accomplished professional photographer.

Ray's Books:

• A book of poetry and lyrics, *Life over a cup of Tea*, was published in 2011.

• His first novel, *The Trojan Towers*, was published in 2005.

• A second political thriller, the first of the Enda Osin Mysteries, *Isia's Secret*, was published in September 2013.

• The next in the series, *Twisted Wire*, was published in September 2014.

• In 2015, Ray published a sequel to *The Trojan Towers*, a chase thriller titled *Crate Of Lies*.

All Ray's works are available in e-version and print.
Audio versions are in production.

Ray's favourite authors:
Charles Dickens, Sir Arthur Conan Doyle, Neville Shute,
Alistair Maclean, C. S. Forrester, Len Deighton,
Daniel Silva, Ernest Hemingway – and the list goes on.

Contact Ray here:

Website: RayStoneAuthor.org
Email: ray@raystoneauthor.com

Twitter: @raystoneauthor?lang=en

Facebook: http://facebook.com/raystoneauthor

Pinterest:

http://pinterest.com/

https://www.pinterest.com/raystone/boards/

Tumblr:

https://www.tumblr.com/blog/raystoneme

Linkedin:

http://linkedin.com/in/ray-stone-a4ab3355

Google+:

http://plus.google.com/u/0/109792329264388980891

Shutterstock:

http://shutterstock.com/g/raymondstone1946

ISIA'S SECRET

https://www.amazon.com/gp/product/B00OUQLJTG/
Search for : *Isia's Secret* by **Ray Stone**

Isia, the girl with a secret, is in love with George, son of shipping magnate Paul Hrisacopolis, who wants to re-ignite civil war on Cyprus. Sensing a chance to party with influential European politicians, Hrisacopolis has offered to transport priceless artifacts from the British Museum on board the flagship of his cruise line.

 However, Hrisacopolis's Turkish shipping agent Ahmet Zeki, who serves two masters as a double agent, is intent on destroying him. And Enda Osin, controversial political columnist for *The Herald,* gets entangled when he begins to research Hrisacopolis, aided by West Indian art correspondent Jessica Du Rosse.

Jessica is beautiful, sophisticated—and half his age—and he's soon falling in love. An unforgettable cruise!

TWISTED WIRE

https://www.amazon.com/gp/product/B00NA916ZG

Search for : *Twisted Wire* by **Ray Stone**

Enda Osin, correspondent for the Herald, loves political intrigue. After receiving a strange telephone message he thinks is for someone else, he is quickly embroiled in murder, industrial espionage, and a race against time to prevent the world's first hyper-speed aircraft from crashing.

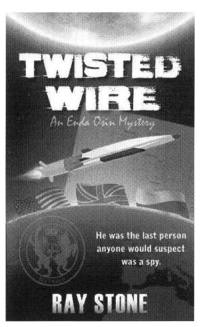

He's soon on the run, with the beautiful Jessica Du Ross and his right-hand man, 'Fish.'

They must elude authorities in several countries, plus Voss, a Russian agent with orders to kill.

In a final double twist, an agent returns to Moscow, Enda sends a gift to the Americans and 'Fish' reveals a shocking secret.

TROJAN TOWERS

https://www.amazon.com/gp/product/B005LDKME0/
Search for : *Trojan Towers* by **Ray Stone**

A priceless icon, crucial to the success of a Middle-Eastern peace deal being secretly brokered by America and Russia, has been stolen. Harry Cohen, London desk for Mossad, recruits Raithe Ravelle, a professional thief, who has just been released on appeal. Ravelle has a score to settle—and it's personal. Harry mentored his daughter Natalie.

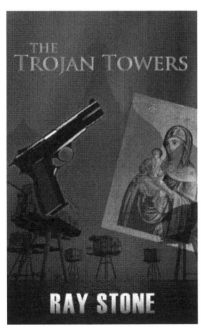

The men plan a daring robbery but, after Natalie is kidnapped, they are in a race against time. After a whirlwind chase through several European cities, their search reaches deserted wartime forts in the River Thames, where they face a life-and-death struggle to reach the frightened teenager—and retrieve the treasure in the Trojan Towers.

CRATE OF LIES

https://www.amazon.com/Crate-Lies-Ray-Stone-ebook/
dp/B015UJZG4U/

Search for : *Crate of Lies* by **Ray Stone**

Harry Cohen, 'London Desk' for Mossad, has found a link
that might lead to Russia's lost Amber Room treasure.
With the aid of his trusted agent, former criminal Raithe
Ravelle, he must trace the secret route the room travelled
and expose an Arab arms-smuggling ring.

Their route is ingenious,
originally devised by SS
General Wilheim Rienecke.
But Moscow is only a step
behind, and has hired ex-
Stasi agent Heinrich Lieb-
ermann to find the Amber
Room first—and eliminate
Harry and Raithe. From
Vladivostok, the trail leads
to Moscow and then through
Minsk, Warsaw, Prague and
Berlin. Nothing is what it
seems until the final page.

LIFE OVER A CUP OF TEA

https://www.amazon.com/gp/product/B005EJF55M/
Search for : *Life Over a Cup of Tea* by **Ray Stone**

A look at life through Ray Stone's eyes — and warped mind.

This eclectic collection of poetry, lyrics and anecdotes - from an englishman living in the USA - is humorous, sad, thoughtful and thought-provoking.

Add some light relief to that time of day when one sips the elixir of life - a cup of tea.

Made in the USA
Monee, IL
24 February 2020